Murphy finds a way to generate an un[...]
acters, as they (alongside we readers) [...]
this world, and the extraordinariness lurking in its carefully observed mundanities; bemused at its ability, in turn, to break and to lift up our hearts. These stories know that one can't ever shake the losses we've endured, but they also know that the act of endurance can be a holy one, that grief and incantation can sometimes twine. The result, as these stories accumulate, is electric and exhilarating. This book made me want to go out into the world, and to look and look and look at all of the magic—melancholy and otherwise—that I hadn't noticed before.

—MATTHEW GAVIN FRANK, author of
Flight of the Diamond Smugglers

Devin Murphy's *Unbend the River* is an antidote for a cynical age. These stories catalog many of the modern maladies that plague fly-over country—addiction, vanished jobs, dissolving families—then take us so deep into the experience that we too pray for mercy along with this cast of misfits. Murphy has a strong eye for detail and an ear attuned to the music of American tongues, and he shows incredible heart as his characters strive to keep each other close.

—THEODORE WHEELER, author of *The War Begins in Paris*

There's something decidedly *autumnal* about Devin Murphy's big-hearted new collection, *Unbend the River*, every character achingly suspended between who they were, and who they'll be—between the seasons that make up a life. And yet who doesn't linger to watch the colors change? Sieved from the Allegheny River, these stories walk right off the page. They loom over your shoulder. They sit in your gut. They haunt you from one room to the next, because these wounded lives, so tenderly wrought, aren't theirs alone. They're ours. Only in Murphy's sure hands would that melancholy sip so neat.

—CARSON VAUGHAN, author of *Zoo, Nebraska: The Dismantling of an American Dream*

Every character in *Unbend the River* feels real and deeply rooted: in a landscape, in a community, in work, in a family or web of friendships, in their own histories and hopes. In these powerfully observed, richly detailed stories, Devin Murphy beautifully explores how the places and people we love can shape, strangle, and ultimately sustain each other.

—CAITLIN HORROCKS, author of *Life Among the Terranauts*

UNBEND
THE
RIVER

UNBEND
THE RIVER

DEVIN MURPHY

BLACK LAWRENCE PRESS

 Black
Lawrence
Press

www.blacklawrence.com

Executive Editor: Diane Goettel
Cover Art: "Unending 3" by Teodora Prodanova
Cover and Interior Design: Zoe Norvell

Published 2024 by Black Lawrence Press.
Printed in the United States.

For Becca, Hyat, Nora, and Jude

Table of Contents

WAITING FOR THE COYWOLF

Ralph is the largest golden retriever to ever live, and you can't tell me any different. His head is enormous, his chest the prow of a rowboat, his heart big enough for me to fit inside it. He's fierce and protective, and despite his size and my fragility, we're good company for each other. Right now we're on a walk around the almost-empty new development beside my home. A couple I've never seen before waves to us from their front yard.

"Hi!" the woman says—to Ralph, not to me.

I stop. I do this often to catch my breath now. "Do you know Ralph?" I ask.

"He joins us for our run every morning," she says.

A trim forty-something man with hair grown out and gelled back over the thin spot pats Ralph's head. Ralph slobbers and croons.

"He runs with you?" I ask.

"Every morning," she says.

"How far?

"We average about four miles," the man says. He stands up and pats his flat stomach proudly.

"*My* dog? My Ralph runs with you?"

"Chases us down and keeps up the whole way," the woman says, talking slow and being sweet. I can tell she's not used to being around old people.

I look at Ralph. When I let him out every morning, I thought he was napping in the yard, but clearly he's been escaping the electric fence and roaming. Ralph pants and smiles, then does a terrific spine bend to chew his own tail.

"Seventy-five dollars to come out there, and seventy-five dollars an hour after that," the electric-dog-fence guy tells me over the phone.

"But you set it up, and it isn't working."

"If you do it yourself, you'll save a lot of money."

"Do what myself?"

"Test the shock collar."

"How?"

"Walk over the line with it."

"What?"

"We do it all the time. It's not that bad."

"I'm eighty-six and have a pacemaker. Do you think I should be giving myself a shock?"

"Well . . . it's seventy-five dollars to come out."

In the morning I step outside with Ralph. He has on the electric collar but runs a big circle around my house to build speed and then barrels over the shock line and takes off—all one hundred twenty pounds of him pumping away like a racehorse, rounding the gardenia bush and lilacs before straightening at the chandelier-pear tree and bolting through the neighborhood toward the woods beyond.

I'm annoyed with the fence company that installed the underground line but strangely happy at the sight of my dog harrumphing out into the world.

My neighborhood in the Southern Tier of New York is a monstrosity of capitalism gone to rot. I bought some forested land here and built my house in the seventies, when things were good for my Whetstone Knife factory. My house sat like a quiet abbey in the woods beside a small creek, and I lived here in peace until seven years ago, when a developer trying to expand on the nearby Chautauqua Institution tourist resort bought the surrounding land, plowed along the ravine to my driveway, and laid a giant circular road with cul-de-sacs hanging off it like Brussels sprouts from a stalk. Most of the lots sold, the houses were custom designed before being built, and sales went well enough that the developer cut a second circle into the forest for a new set of McMansions. Then the recession hit, and half the houses went unfinished or were sold cheap to people who could never otherwise afford the square footage. Then housing values climbed again, and those people got buried under property taxes and foreclosed. Now every other yard has a wooden realtor sign pounded into the ground. I can see nine houses from my front yard: Four are for sale under dubious circumstances. The hodgepodge of remainders make up my neighbors.

Ilene died the year after the developers showed up. Part of me blames them. I know it's ridiculous, but it gives me a place to aim my anger and disappointment.

Ralph pants back in the late morning. I remove his shock collar, which emits a beeping sound within four feet of the fence line. I'm afraid to go any closer and risk a shock that might monkey with whatever natural current runs through me—though another part of me, in a place too deep to name, is ready to have that inner current shocked flat and be done with it.

I walk around the east side of the house, where the last unbroken wall of forest is still standing before the drop into the ravine. I stop at the lawn chair and sit. I sometimes sit here at night when I can't sleep. Last month I saw a giant coyote at the tree line. Big as a black bear. I've been waiting to get another look at it ever since. I've read about a new creature called a "coywolf"—the offspring of a coyote and a timber wolf. That must have been what I saw. Waiting for it to reappear gives me something to do.

I stand up and trace the route of Ralph's charge around the house, close to the fence line. I'm just about to cross the line, electric collar in hand—it will look like an accident, an honest mistake—when I hear, "Hi, Bruce."

I look up. Eddy, the neighbor boy, is in his yard, staring at me through the lilacs I planted to create a buffer between me and the succession of buyers who've trounced through next door.

"Hi, Eddy," I say.

"What are you doing?" he asks, looking at the collar.

"I was going to shock myself."

"Why?" He's an acorn-squash-shaped boy with a unibrow. Nine. Ten. Maybe eleven. His T-shirt has some new-age superhero punching some new-age villain. Eddy emerges from the lilacs and gets a tongue bath from Ralph, who must have a hard time living alone with me, as he will give his love to anyone.

"Would you like to give it a try for me?" I say to Eddy.

"Sure." He comes closer, happy to do whatever I ask.

"No, no. I'm joking." No way am I going to test the fence with this boy here. I picture myself lighting up and rattling three inches off the ground, then dropping dead in front of Eddy, and I let out a little laugh.

"What's the joke?" Eddy asks.

"Joke's on me," I say, and I hook the collar back on Ralph.

At six that night the doorbell rings. It's Eddy's mother, Melissa. She's got the sort of trim body middle-aged women get from smoking and not eating, which leaves their faces looking tired and slack, like age is pulling them into the earth by their cheeks.

"Mr. Ferguson," she says, "I was hoping you could help our family out."

"You name it," I say, all charm and spice, like a silly idiot. I open the door wide to let her in and have to hold Ralph back from putting his nose between her legs. "Don't mind him," I say and lead her into my living room. We sit in twin rocking chairs Amish carpenters made for me from trees removed to clear the lot for my home.

Eddy's dad, Lenwood, is an obese wheezer with a scar-dappled neck. He owns a shady bar near Olean called The Tavern, which I'm told has a one-eyed woman tending bar, like a proper pirate establishment. Eddy's mom, Melissa, has an event-planning job and works odd hours. They're the fourth owners of the home next door in seven years. Often they turn the music up at night and drunkenly smash plates and flip tables without any mind to the boy probably tucked away in one corner or another of that giant house. From time to time they let their little white squirrel of a dog, Pearl, outside, where she pees, yips at shadows, and scratches to be let back inside. I think Pearl knows the coywolf is out there and is afraid.

"So, how can I help you?" I ask Melissa.

"Well, Pearl is diabetic and needs insulin shots. Sometimes, when we can't make it home in time for her shots, she pees all over the house. We were hoping you wouldn't mind giving her the shots on days we can't make it?"

I laugh—a coming-to-my senses laugh, a pretty-women-don't-do-much-for-me-anymore laugh. Melissa stares at me like I'm mad. I don't think she likes my laughing at her request. I don't think she likes me, period, but it's no loss. I look at her and the house she lives in as invasive species.

I hold up my hand, jittery as a drunk's. "The only shot you'd want me giving her is a lethal one, because sure enough that would be the result."

At night I sit in my chair near the dark woods. I often hear distant gunfire, which I always told Ilene was the mating call of the local rednecks. Now I wonder about all the lives in the region and how the people here get by. Who do they live for? Who do they have to live without? It's also easy for me to daydream about early settlers building forges along the river. The Indian guides first leading people west through here and into Ohio. How the Franciscans for some reason ended up founding a college here. The history draws me in, like now, I need some fuller sense of the place I've spent my life.

The mosquitos whizz around my head but find nothing in me worth taking. Sometimes I wonder if I imagined the coywolf, if my old eyes and new fears conjured her out of the shadows. I think I am trying to make a place for wonder in my life. Or maybe I have slipped off the deep end. Who knows? The coywolf had huge yellow eyes. She and I understood each other. I want Ralph to mate with her and breed golden-oyte pups, wild yellow scavengers to populate the woods and drive the developers and backhoes away.

Don't go back there, I'll tell the workers. *There's golden-yotes roaming around those woods.* I picture wolf-retrievers loping out of the underbrush with deer femurs between their jaws. My mind has gone soft with age, but I'm near giddy with the image of Ralph's wild offspring: joyous, cagey, snappy creatures.

I hear Eddy and his mother and father clattering around the huge house they can afford only because it's lost most of its value. I see Melissa step outside with Pearl. A red jewel of a lit cigarette draws closer to her face, flares, and fades.

When she goes back inside, the yelling starts. I can hear the tone, not the words. They're in the middle years of life, where some seem to lean back and let go of the reins.

They will smash into a tree before too long. For Eddy's sake, I hope the trunk has some give to it.

Jessie Roberts, who lives alone in a giant house on the other side of the development's circle, is on his bike again and peddling at high speed with his iPhone strapped to the crossbars and its speaker repeating the same phrase over and over: "I told you you were going to be sorry. I told you you were going to be sorry. I told you you—"

The voice belongs to an angry woman with a Russian accent. I've been told it's a voicemail from his ex-wife, Anastasia. He pedals like he's on an Olympic trial run, pumping out all the vitriol coursing through him. He goes by so fast and with such fury that sometimes I hear only part of the message "I told . . ." Then, about seven minutes later, ". . . you you . . ." This repeats as it gets darker, like the land is accusing us of something. Of our mere presence.

On the main road leading to the commuter highway, there's a pull-off where a cider stand sets up shop in mid-August. They keep a small leaf pile burning during business hours so that the deep earth and ash smell floats on the cool air and reminds us of change and makes us want to drink warm apple juice and eat sugary doughnuts. Ralph and I oblige. I drive my 1931 Cadillac Fleetwood V16 that I bought from a local muscle-head mechanic named Sugar to the cider stand when it's busy. There people stop to admire the car and pet Ralph and feed him doughnuts. Ralph wags his tail. I like the attention for him and the car. We sit there all morning. It's something to do. Sometimes Ralph looks up at planes leaving trails in the sky. Maybe he thinks it's a spider caught on a breeze with a glowing silk thread dragging taut behind it. Maybe he smells someone he could love up there. His heart is so big, I put nothing past him.

When I get home from the doughnut stand, the boy, Eddy, is in my house. On my couch. Watching TV.

"Hi, Eddy."

"Hi, Bruce."

"How's it going?"

"Good."

"What are you doing?"

"Watching TV."

"So you just came over?"

"Yes."

"Are your parents home?"

"No."

"Do they know you're here?"

"They told me to come over and play with Ralph if I'm alone."

"They did?"

"Yes."

He's watching nimble adults in colored leotards and cartoonish helmets have karate battles with strange puppets. Ralph puts his huge head on the boy's lap and whacks the coffee table with his tail.

"Don't you have anything better to do?" I ask.

"I go to science camp on Tuesdays and Thursdays," Eddy says, as if this explains everything.

"Are you hungry, Eddy?"

"I'm always hungry. My mom says I have a tapeworm."

"Well, have some doughnuts then."

I sit next to the boy. I have no idea what else to do.

Eddy the boy, Ralph the dog, and I spend the next hour eating doughnuts and watching television. At one point Eddy gets up and walks right to the bathroom without even asking where it is, like he's grown up in this house. Later he walks to the window that looks toward his home. When he comes back to the couch, he's holding a picture frame.

"Is this your wife?" Eddy asks.

In the picture Ilene is standing in front of the lake at Allegany State Park. Her eyes are a shimmering blue. They made me dizzy when we were young.

"Can you please put that back where you found it."

"OK," Eddy says. I watch him put the picture back on the shelf full of local crafts and tchotchkes that Ilene bought at the annual arts fair.

"Are your parents home now?" I ask.

"Looks like it."

"Won't they be missing you?"

"Sure." He pats Ralph's head and goes to the door. Before he steps out, he looks back at me. "I had a nice time, Bruce."

To kill the rest of the afternoon, I go to the Olean Public Library. Years ago Ilene made me donate money for books, and the library purchased a collection of travel books in my name. I don't know if anyone has ever read them, but I am reading them now. I thumb through a book on India and its folklore, which fascinates me. Of all the places on earth I won't make it to, India would offer the largest culture shock.

Then I read about sheep ranchers in Colorado who take Great Pyrenees pups and wrap them in freshly shorn wool. That way, when the dogs meet the sheep, they take to them right away. I imagine wrapping them in wolf fur, putting them in a wolf den, and waiting until they come out of the woods to feast upon the sheep.

I take my time getting home, going for a drive along the Allegheny River, which is as lovely and interesting as any place on earth. When I get back, I work in the garden. My body is a wreck, heavy and slow, but I love the dark smell of upturned earth. It helps distract me from thoughts of playing chicken with the shock fence.

"Need some help, Bruce?" Eddy calls from his yard.

I look up at his wide, expectant face. "Don't you have a bike or something? Ride to a park. Play sports. With other kids."

"That's OK. I can help you for a bit." He walks closer, and Ralph begins dancing crotch-sniffing circles around him as soon as he passes the lilacs.

"Well. Find a weed and pull it I guess."

He starts pacing beside the flower bed. "How about this one?" He holds up a wilted Asiatic lily.

"No, not those."

"It looks dried up."

"Look here," I say, and I dig around the base of the wilting lily, using my trowel and then my fingers to brush away dirt and expose the bulb. "The bulb pulls the energy back from the dying leaves. That way it can grow strong again." I feel good to have taught him something.

"OK, Bruce."

"I used to dig up buckets of mud from the banks of the river to fertilize this garden," I tell him. "It worked so well the flowers damn near hit orbit. Tulips the size of boxing gloves. Deer were crazy for them."

Eddy laughs.

At night I'm tired, but I don't sleep. I'm not haunted by anything—except yesterday, I suppose, when I almost tried to stop my heart.

I go sit by the woods and look for the coywolf, and I hear Eddy's parents, Lenwood and Melissa, holler at each other. I feel sorry for Eddy. His home must be a scary place to live.

On the last weekend of summer, the Olean water park does a good deed, a mitzvah for mutts: before they drain and clean the huge pool, they let locals bring their dogs to run loose and swim.

"Go get Pearl," I tell Eddy, who's lingering at the edge of the lilacs, waiting for me to invite him over.

Once Eddy's buckled into the back seat of the Cadillac with Pearl on his lap, Ralph jumps in and slaps Eddy across the brow with his tail. On the drive to the park, we get stuck behind a garbage truck with a sticker that says, IF YOU ARE NOT SATISFIED WITH OUR SERVICE, DOUBLE YOUR TRASH BACK.

At the water park I take a handicap spot, and though the pool is full and the man at the gate is turning away dog owners and their pooches, I limp up with turnip-headed Eddy and his puny dog and my giant golden dragging my bag of bones, and I lay it on thick, like this single event will make my long life complete. Finally the gate flunky takes pity on us and lets us in.

Almost two hundred neighborhood dogs play in the water and around the pool deck. The sand pit for kids looks like a small dust cloud from all the dogs digging in there. Several have dug so deep that all I can see is their wagging tails.

I sit in a folding chair and unhook Ralph, who bolts into the fray. "What about Pearl?" I say.

"I'm not sure she'll like this," Eddy says, but he unclips the overgrown ferret, who cowers under my chair. When a poodle sniffs her,

Pearl lies down and goes belly-up.

"Don't be so meek," I say to the dog. To the boy.

Ralph is sprinting in and out of the water, barking, barking, barking. He stops to hump a Great Dane. He gets good and into it before the Great Dane's owners huff over and pull my piston-hipped dog away.

The air smells like chlorine and wet fur. Ralph runs off and gets lost in the crowd of random breeds. I catch glimpses of him: Halfway up the roped-off waterslide stairs. Swimming circles in the deep end. Sniffing asses. Jumping up and licking a young man's face. Humping a Saint Bernard. He has a thing for dogs bigger than him, pays no mind to ones who are clearly inferior in mind, body, and spirit.

Pearl never leaves the shadow of my chair.

"Look at that one," Eddy keeps saying, happy to be watching such a mess. I have to admit it makes me happy, too.

Ralph's exhausted on the drive back. Eddy can't stop talking. When we pull into my driveway, he leans over the front seat.

"What do you like about me?" Eddy asks. As if we're a young couple in love. As if I owe him some kind of ode to his beauty. I look at his yard to see if his mother is there to summon the boy. She isn't. I need to come up with an answer, something meaningful to tell him. There's a reason he asked this.

"I like your spirit," I say. "I think you could run with the wolves if you wanted. I think your heart's big enough to hold the whole world."

I turn away from him. From his need. I don't think this makes me a bad person. Well, maybe it does.

The skinny trees in the lawns of the empty houses are starting to turn. Fall is upon us. Then comes winter, one long sheet of gray in this part of the country. It gets so cold the ground freezes solid. Ice crystals make glowing religious symbols on the ribs of fallen leaves. Part of me is certain I will not make it through February. It's the first time such a feeling has come to me with an approximate date attached. I'm OK with this. I'm OK with going back to the source of the garden. Pearl the diabetic dog will pee on my dirt. I think again of taking Ralph's collar and crossing the shock line to get it over with.

"Do you ever wish Ralph could walk on two legs like a man?" Eddy asks from the lilacs as I walk along the shock line, beeping collar in hand. I didn't know he was behind me. My fist is sweating over the collar. The two steel prongs meant for the dog's throat make indents on my skin.

"No," I say.

"I do."

Eddy follows me to my lawn chair, and I sit down. His unibrow needs to be tended to. I imagine other kids tease him because of it.

"Sometimes I also wish squirrels were fifty pounds. That would be more interesting."

"How's that?"

"If they were bigger, people would have to stay away from them. A fifty-pound squirrel jumping around in the trees is nothing to joke about."

"I suppose it isn't," I say. "Did you learn that at science camp this week?"

"We learned about Yellowstone National Park. They said it smells bad."

"What does?"

"The gushers at Yellowstone."

"Geysers."

"Yeah, geysers. They said it's from the sulfur in the water. Smells like a skunk farting after eating bad eggs." He laughs. A boy's humor. Ralph appears and pushes his giant head between Eddy's legs and lifts him into the air.

Eddy's parents come home later. A car door slams. Pearl barks. I'm outside holding the shock collar like a talisman. I like to think about a wild animal circling me from the deepest woods. Coming closer. Closer. It's taken on a life of its own in my head.

I fall asleep in the lawn chair and wake to the sound of Eddy screeching in pain. He's by the electric fence line and shaking his left arm like he's trying to fling off some sort of hot putty.

"Damn it," I say. "Get away from that."

"This really works," Eddy says, holding up the black collar.

In the morning I let Ralph out and watch him pee on the flowers, sniff the yard, then gallop around the house and through the electric fence. He runs down the road to join the joggers.

I'm about to go back inside when I hear the shovel blade hit. Eddy's father is digging a hole behind their house. Next to him is something wrapped in a beach towel.

"Morning, Lenwood," I call, and he damn near drops the shovel in surprise. "Didn't mean to give you a coronary," I say.

He steps in front of the beach towel.

"Burying your wife's head this morning?" I ask.

"I guess it could look like that, huh."

"One piece at a time. That's a good strategy," I say. Whatever the hell he's doing, it's the first time I've seen him up so early, and I want to mess with him. I guess because I don't like him. I've never seen him do anything with Eddy. I've never seen him engage with his son in any meaningful way. "Sure does look like you're about to plant your wife's severed head."

Lenwood laughs. This man looks like he was once strong but had that power taken away somehow, beaten or drained out of him.

"We lost Pearl last night," he says.

"You *lost* her?"

"Well . . . it's sort of a mess."

I stare at the towel and wish I hadn't said anything.

"We drank a bit too much, and before bed I gave Pearl her shot, because she pees all over the rug without it."

"Right."

"Then Pearl was barking, and Melissa thought I hadn't given her the shot. So she went down and gave her another."

Insulin shock.

Lenwood bends down and grabs the shovel. "We drank too much, you know? Who was thinking about it?" His hands on the brown shovel handle look pale and soft. I can tell he's sick from a hangover. "I'm trying to do this before Eddy wakes up," he says.

When Eddy comes over in the afternoon, I can see he's been crying. I don't ask about Pearl. Dogs die in this life. He knows this now, so I say nothing. What I do is I help him with his science project. He follows me to the garage to look for materials. We find a box of embroidery supplies, a pair of tennis rackets, and boxes of magazines Ilene subscribed to that I kept but have never gotten around to reading.

"What's this?" Eddy asks. He holds up a spool that I wound miles of kite string on years ago, when I was trying out hobbies. It took hours to wind it all up.

"Focus," I tell Eddy. He's supposed to do a demonstration of the wind's power.

We end up making a tornado out of gray and white streamers that we hang from a hula-hoop and cinch at the bottom, so it looks like a twister. We suspend the hoop from a ladder and tape a few of his action figures into the streamers. Behind it we place a fan and a chalkboard easel with thunderclouds and lightning drawn on it. When we're done, we turn on the fan, switch off all the lights in my living room, and use flashlights to strobe lightning strikes over our little funnel cloud.

Ralph barks when the tornado starts to sway.

I think I'm going to die in February, and this is what I've done with my day.

I see Eddy's mother smoking a cigarette behind her house.

"I'll be right back, bud."

Ralph thumps his tail. Eddy says nothing.

The mother's still going for sexy and stylish but looks wispy and tired. Her arms are folded over her stomach, fingers kneading her elbows, making little circles over the bone. When I approach, she drops her half-smoked cigarette into the grass.

"I thought maybe you'd be interested in knowing where Eddy is. Should I give him dinner?"

"No. I'll come get him."

"He seems a bit lonely."

"Oh?"

"I'm not the best company. I'm pretty old."

"He likes your dog."

"Well, the dog isn't a good babysitter."

She doesn't respond. I go home and come back with Eddy. Ralph follows us across the lawn. The boy's mother is still standing in the same spot, making those small circles around her elbows. Her face is red, like shame is peeling her open.

Eddy glances at her with a flash of anger before he swallows those feelings down. Something collapses inside me when I see how practiced he is at hiding hurt, how full of negative feelings he must be. I've underestimated him. I want to weep for the future of Eddy the boy. This woman will ruin all measure of sweetness in him. I feel like I've failed him, ushered him back to his parents' self-hatred, his loneliness, that giant, ugly home.

Before Eddy and Melissa go into their house, I say, "Wait a minute. I could use Eddy's help for something else, if he has time."

"I do," Eddy says.

"Is it OK with your mom?"

Eddy looks up at his mother, who reaches out to cup her hand against his cheek. She nods, and Eddy bolts back to me.

In the garage I have Eddy get the giant spool and a kite. We climb into the Cadillac with Ralph, drive to the highest part of the unde-veloped development, and get out. Eddy has to help me up the incline. From here we can see the rolling hills and the first hint of fall colors.

I hook the kite to the reel.

"You get it hoisted up there," I tell Eddy. He raises the kite. When the wind comes up the backside of the hill and takes it from his hand, I hit the lever so the string starts spooling out, out, out. It picks up speed and rises fast.

"How high will it go?" Eddy asks.

"We've got to be careful not to hook a big ol' airliner," I tell him.

"Damn near hitting orbit now," Eddy says, and he gives me a stupid grin.

"That's right, buddy."

Jessie Roberts rounds the corner on his bike with the voice of his ex-wife belittling him.

Ralph has taken our lack of attention as permission to run for it, the yellow flash of him darting toward joggers on the distant bend.

I watch the kite ascend and imagine looking down on this place from that high up, seeing where I've lived most of my life—my radiant energy lingering, a bioluminescence trailing off like morning mist.

Eddy looks up at the sky. I want to tell him something, something worthwhile, but nothing comes to me. So I start telling him about the wild coywolf circling the woods as the kite keeps rising.

SUGAR AND PRISCILLA

Sugar and Priscilla climbed through each other's windows.

Priscilla crosses the wraparound porch of her Victorian house, past the horse barn, pastures, and hitching post where tourists start their horse rides. She walks barefoot over County Road C to Sugar's gravel driveway, the giant barn where he and his father, Henry, rehab old cars, past the first abandoned trailer, the two abandoned trailers linked together in a T in front of the cow pasture, and to the trailer the two men now share. Around her the loosening buds of soy plants and the next corn crop crack open the earth. The clear glittering of stars marks her passage from bed to bed. In the dark they sleep entwined, belly to back or belly to belly, until the first slanting pillars of sun sweep the corners of the room, and they separate, she becoming a shadow crossing the road once more.

The next night, he'll make the trip to her window.

At first, during their junior year of Olean High School, they were fumbling and awkward with each other. Though, with time, they became confident in the aerobic feats of youth. It was over those years that Prissy watched Samuel Bergman become Sugar. It was a slow transition after he began working on his body, heaving the old rusted weights in the garage around, until his shoulders stretched out like an ox yoke, the washboard abs protruded like angry knots, his pectoral muscles curved out hard and smooth as frozen turkeys. Then the tattoos came. A demon car driving up his right calf muscle. A buffalo at the back of his neck. The barbed wire ring around his left bicep, a dozen more, some with bright reds, and blues, and others deep blacks. Finally, the bold block lettering of *S.U.G.A.R.* making an arch over his belly button. His blond hair grew shaggy, then wild, then straightened with length and was pulled into a ponytail. There were times he sat out in the sun and turned the color of a skinned olive. Then there were winter months he drove to Buffalo to tanning beds and his skin yellowed, a copper gold that made him look jaundiced and sick. Often he'd lather his chest and neck in baby oil so he glistened. He had taken whatever old misery he inherited from his mother's departure and turned it into his body, into his cars.

At times Prissy felt by touch alone she could loosen that sadness from his body, let it free, and perhaps she did, as it was a silent pull, a need for touch, that culled them from their sleep. Then, after years, it was habit. The seasons governed their coupling. During the late spring or early summer, when the neighboring town of Chautauqua started filling up with seasonal workers at the art institute, they'd try their luck with strangers, each enthralled for the short season by the otherness of their prospects, until repeated letdowns pulled them back together. To Sugar, Prissy had become a seasonal bird, heading off in the warm weather, doubling back in the cold.

At the mailbox in the cold morning air, Sugar thumbed through another stack of medical bills for his gimped father, a thick, bro-ken-hearted diabetic with grease caked into the grooves of his callused hands. There was also an *Easyriders* magazine with tattooed beauties sprawled over the polished chrome hoods of hot rods. Sugar enjoyed seeing the beauties, but was disappointed again for not receiving the letter he wanted. He had adapted the fuel injection system of an old Mustang so that he could improve the performance of the hybrid engine, and hoped that he had found a way to improve *all* engines. Now he stood at the mailbox every day waiting for the letter from the patent office. He was certain his designs would be the start of his future. He'd find money to stake a factory or sell the design outright at an auction to a major car manufacturer. It was the avenue to change his life, his father's life, Prissy's life. Though with the deep freezes swooning down from Canada, zippering up the center of the state with ice, and his request still not garnering a response, he'd begun to doubt himself. He had made a tweak, sure. But he hadn't *invented* anything and now he wondered if tweaking counted for anything at all.

The dew was still heavy on the uncut grass by the side of the road. Sugar looked for Prissy across the street. Her hair pulled into a ponytail. Jeans cinched tight over her hips. He could burn up thinking of her body and felt he might ignite right there on the road. When he hadn't crossed the road for a long time, the thought of her leaving this place began to fester and sunk an inner strength he had always counted on. If she ever left for good, which she desperately wanted to do, he knew there would be a real down in his life. *The* down. Something he couldn't get over.

There had been dozens of reasons for her to leave in the past. And even now, she could love someone and follow him off, the way Sugar's mother had. Or her horse show gets discovered and that carries her off, or she finally runs out of money to pay the operating cost of her senile grandfather's horse ranch and has to leave, or, or, or.

Sugar walked back up the driveway, past the four trailers to the barn, where he sat and watched Prissy from the entrance of his barn as she went about working with the horses. She led the horses out to paddock to let them graze and run. Then she cleaned the stalls, scooping the wet and fecund hay into a wheelbarrow and dropping it into a waste pile behind the shed. She climbed the steep steel stairwell to the loft and tossed down stacks of fresh hay bales from the rafters to the ground. Then she gripped the ladder railing, kicked her feet over the bars, and slid down like a Navy serviceman, a trick she'd been doing since she was a girl. When the new hay was spread and the trough full of clean water, she'd ready the horses in the pasture for a day of touring. Only a third of the horses got saddled for stop-in guests, mostly second-home owners from Chautauqua with their grandchildren. Some horses were left to graze in the paddocks by the road so passing drivers would see the array of animals. She listened to the sound of water sucking down the drain and the deep, snorting breath of the horses as she sponged them down from the sudsy bucket, running her hands back and forth along their flanks.

When the stalls were cleaned, she'd start on the ponies, walking them for a half hour so they got used to being led by a bit. With rubber slicker boots she led them along the corn fields beyond her property. Then she walked around the soy that rose and dipped all the way over a dozen farms until the highway cut a path several miles to the north. When the ponies were warmed up, she put them in the pen and ran them in circles on a lead to get a sweat up, before really working them. She got them running and bucking their energy loose in wild kicks and the stamping of their hooves. It was at this stage, when they were young and wild and didn't know their own power, that she loved working with them most. Their unbridled ability and personalities started to reveal themselves. Most would break early and get sent to the stable and dressed each morning to spend a life carrying tourists and their children in slow-moving, single-file lines around the planting fields and foothills. Or, and it was rare enough that she had to kindle the hope of it happening by daydreaming about it, the horse would be stubborn, wild, have that ancient meanness that she would have to fight and fight so that when it finally did offer its submission, it would be total, and she would be able to wield its power to do anything. Those were the animals she loved most. Those were the ones she could see herself on, translating messages with her hands, slipping from high on the shoulders to a long hold low on the horse's back, making the creature move the way she wanted it to before the movement even formed in her own mind, a melding of muscle and heartbeat into grace and motion. Those were the horses she dreamed of. Those were the one's she named after the Iroquois-speaking Wenrohronon tribe that first lived here.

Henry came out sipping from a tin can with steam rising off the brim. He'd stayed out late watching his friends play in the over fifty men's ice hockey league in town. He limped into the garage with a thick oak cane beside him because he had mangled half his foot in a motorcycle accident as a young man. Now, diabetes was gnawing at his other leg from the knee down with doctors wanting to take the second foot, the good foot. Doctors wanted him to pay fortunes for this sectioning off of his humanity and for prosthetics that would keep him mobile.

Henry pointed to the mail.

"Didn't get your letter?"

"Nope."

"Wasting your time, boy." Henry was spreading seeds around

the ground near his pigeon coop. Since Sugar's mother ran off with a summer vacationer almost twenty years earlier, Henry kept a pigeon coop behind the barn. He tied little notes to their gnarled feet and sent them off into the sky. Sugar never looked at the notes and never asked what his father was sending up into the air. He figured his father needed to float some language away from his own heart and let those messages do their roundtrips from the pigeon house, untouched by him.

"You think any of those big auto places will want to make their cars better?" Henry asked. "They've probably got the technology locked up for cars that will last a century so they don't go out of business. Wasting your time with that hope."

They were working on a flood-damaged and abandoned '65 Shelby Mustang salvaged from a dump in Olean. Sugar made most of his money with cars. Dozens of long drives a year along the Rustbelt, out to Iowa, and then to the upper Midwest into northern Wisconsin and Minnesota, across the Upper Peninsula in Michigan and down under the lake through Gary, Indiana, and the outlying Chicago junkyards created a network of friends who knew to call him when they came across the husks of older model cars or the spare parts for such unique vehicles. He'd recently rehabbed the shells of a gangster's 1920 Packard Twin Six and a 1931 Cadillac Fleetwood V16. There had been dozens of muscle cars with their menacing slant from the front hood to their raised chrome spoiler, roadsters and sporting coupes flattened in highway crashes mostly. Using the cable crank, he pulled the cars aboard the flatbed truck and loaded any remaining surface area of the trailer with spare parts he knew he could sell to the owners of cars he'd built.

There was always some new task unfolding in the garage. Over the years, Henry and Sugar could communicate through machine parts, injection nozzles, vacuum pumps, spark plugs. They took the husk of some dead old car and revived it so it could tear hell over the back roads, a chrome flash across the Southern Tier Highway, tracking the Allegheny River until it dips south into Pennsylvania. The deep rumble or slow wheeze of the engine pumping away according to how they set the pitch of the exhaust and muffler. The garage always rattled with potential for Sugar, and as an adult, he only felt whole, like he was growing toward something, when he was working on cars. The cars became an art form. He worked on each as if it were some holy tenant of change. A display of skill, power, and beauty that could carry him, or some lucky stranger, into new lives.

Prissy walked in waving a letter in front of her face. "Well, that backfired. The reassessment raised our taxes even more. Now what am I going to do?" She watched Sugar and Henry tinkering on the Shelby and sat on a bench in the garage and cried as they worked. The pigeons whorled in their cage on the backside of the barn.

"I wish those birds weren't so damn loud," Prissy said.

"It's a worthy hobby," Henry said. "Ten thousand years people have been taming these birds."

"Well, maybe ten thousand years ago people could make some money with them. Can you? Can you make us some money with those damn things?" She got up and walked out of the barn. "We're screwed, you know that, right?"

"I can get extra work," Sugar called after her. He'd taken part time and seasonal work cutting trees for Bill Harrison's Lumber Company, running the ski lift at Holiday Valley, bartending at The Tavern, and picking up fill-in shifts at the Whetstone Knife factory. "I'll look for something."

When the Shelby was done, Sugar put an ad in the paper and parked it by the road with a *For Sale* sign in the windshield. For a while, all the old white men at the Chautauqua Institution and Golf Resort were driving his cars. They parked them on the lawn at the ski resort every Sunday and popped the hoods of the vehicles he had pulled from scrap heaps, resurrected, so they could polish the engines and pretend to have built the cars themselves. A bright green Plymouth, an orange Sunbird with a tail fin, a red 1931 Ford Roadster, a soft blue '63 Grand Prix, a chrome green '67 Ford Galaxy convertible. There were '57 Chevys, a forest green VW Karmann Ghia, and a blue '67 Camaro he'd named "Evil Jane."

There were spells when the old men from the resort walked up his driveway and placed orders beforehand, and then the money was good. It was times like that he daydreamed about flying to Cuba, where there were endless old cars fighting off rusting into the earth. He imagined an assembly line of vintage vehicles rolling into a garage where he would bring them back to some exhibitionist's glory, turn each out of his garage, and pile wads of cash away in a safe. But for the last several years the cars sold less frequently, and he'd had to bring in money working day jobs.

The summer brought tourist work to Chautauqua, with gluts of fishermen's pickups dragging flat-hauled bass boats for the weekend. Vacationers brought speed boats from Lake Erie, rented slips at the marinas, and filled the hotels and lodges, or owned the million-dollar homes around the lake and collectively created a need for people to work the registers at the tourist shops, wait the tables at the restaurants, and serve drinks at the bars. Every summer a retired astronaut kept his yellow twin engine bi-plane there and swept through the air almost every day, its wings cutting a strange alphabet on the skyline in swooping curls and tightly-arched turns. He hired someone from out of town to stand guard of his plane at night. The locals, who lived in neighboring Olean and Allegheny, or on large tracks of rural land like Sugar and Prissy, were left to cobble lives together for themselves with small seasonal paychecks.

The main tourist attraction in the southern tier was the Dancing Horses Show, which did a performance for stands full of parents and their daughters two times a day all summer. The owners of the Dancing Horses Show had hired Prissy to work the stables when she was a teenager. She showed a flair for working with the horses, which she had grown up around, and she was allowed to be in the show, taking on larger and larger roles until she was training the dancing horses, working her way up to being the star performer, pirouetting the animals in front of the crowd beneath the lights.

After the reassessed tax bill came, Prissy had anyone she could find come to her dancing horse show and film her segment. Her old grandfather, Per, had tried, but he shot more of the crowd's reaction, the dark corners of the building, and a long, uninterrupted stretch of his own lap than anything else. Henry filmed her one night. He came back home and told Sugar about the show.

"Those girls in the audience were transfixed by her. She kills the men, too. Men die watching her body rub against the saddle. You better lock that down, boy."

On the nights Sugar filmed her act, before he was lost in the glow of her skintight sequined bodysuit, he imagined flipping the camera off. He knew talent agents in Hollywood and Los Angeles wanted video mash-ups of skilled animal handlers, and he didn't want to share Prissy with anyone who might take her away. *The thing wouldn't work. Battery died. I thought I was recording.* He voiced the excuses in his head, but filmed anyway. It was always clear that Prissy would float away from this place. The collective glow of the

spotlights on her were going to lift her into the air, allow her to levitate off the ground. Knowing she would leave was the real barrier
that kept him from being totally consumed by her.

Afterward, he sat with Prissy at her bedroom desk as she digitally
sliced the clips together. She spent most of July creating newspapers
inserts and flyers for schools. She planned to send those same flyers
along with the ten-minute video clip she was working on. When
it was done, she had Sugar, Henry, and Per watch in her living
room. She sat on the floor with Lobo, her giant black-and-white
Newfoundland dog.

In the video, the spotlight swept over the warehouse floor. Then
it snapped off, and back on. Steady now, the light held Prissy on the
back of an unsaddled white horse with three other unsaddled white
horses behind her. They all faced the spotlights, motionless except for
the heavy, heaving breaths lifting the horses' flanks and rippling the
muscles along their backs and shoulders. Then the light flashed off
and in the moment of darkness that passed, Maiden Priscilla, as she
was known, had somehow managed to get all four horses running in
furious circles around the ring. Twenty flood lights flashed on from
every corner of the building, and this wild woman rode atop the lead
horse's shoulders with her arms out to her side. Then she leaned all the
way back so her spine zippered along the ridge of the horse's back and
her lean, graceful legs rose into the air. At a full gallop, Prissy arched
herself into an inverted crescent, then into a locked-elbow handstand.
Steady. Unmoving as the horse carried her in a full circle around the
ring. Then with the four white horses still circling, she tilted off the
back of the horse. The crowd let out a collective gasp. She stuck the
landing, and with subtly bent knees, which she instantly locked, stuck
out one arm which caught the neck of the next charging horse, and
before the horse was done coming out of its turn, she was standing

straight up on its back, arms wide, a big, perfect smile for the crowd. The little girls in the crowd were amazed. Their fathers ogled. Prissy leapt from Wenrohronon-named horse to horse, performing jumping feats, curling and stretching into the characters of some graceful, secret language written only by the body.

The camera spliced to a slow-motion moment of Prissy in mid-air, levitating in the spotlights, not falling or rising. Then the camera sped up and a charging white horse ran beneath her. She jumped from the back of one moving horse to the next. Bounded from the dirt to the animal, then, as quickly as the movement had started, she was in the center of the ring with one horse, the other three circling her. The horse she rode bowed to the crowd, backed up and whipped its body around in circles. Stopped. Reared up on its hind legs and began taking small pounding jumps around the ring. The other three horses stopped, slowed, trotted, and then leapt up on their hind legs and all four horses fell into a small, tight, jumping circle, eventually closing the gap so one's forehooves were on the back of the other, and Prissy rode the circling tonnage of horses and beamed at the crowd.

"Well?" she said, staring at the three men on the couch when her video clip ended.

"What's that, dear?" Per said.

"Well. What do you two think?" she asked Henry and Sugar.

Henry slapped his giant paw on Sugar's knee. "Looks like our girl is going to be headed to Hollywood soon."

"Oh Jesus. Please tell me what you really think of this."

Sugar looked at Prissy and nodded. "You are perfect. They'll see it," he said. What he really wanted to say was, *Please don't leave.* He loved her. He wanted to tell her that so badly now, but was certain that if he revealed himself fully he would spread his arms, lean into her, and crash.

"Oh, my God, I hope so." She lay back down with her head on Lobo's stomach. In the ring, with the horses, there was no need to be a star, no need to be someone else more successful. In motion, on the muscled backs and shoulders of the animals, she felt alive, herself, and the world was beautiful. But when she wasn't with the horses, when she was in her life, with a pile of bills, her ability with the horses felt like something sad, obsolete. A remnant of Wild Bill performances. Some Americana leftover, the vestige of a Highway 66 sideshow.

"Right now, this is all I have to show for myself," she said and held up a flyer for the Dancing Horses Show with her in costume standing on a white horse. "A picture no one will remember."

"Is it the place that makes them dream like this?" Henry asked Per on the couch after watching Prissy's video. Per dabbed at his wet eyes with the cuff of his washed-out flannel shirt. He was looking out the window at the sectioned-off paddocks and the horses. All those horses, generations of horses.

"Have you ever been to Norway?" Per asked.

"Not again, Grandpa," Prissy said. She and Sugar left the room. Henry patted Per on the knee and let him tell his story again.

For his honeymoon, Per took his new bride, his first wife, an eighteen-year-old blond girl named Marda Nurval, on a passage on the Bergen Railway, over the top of Scandinavia, which to them seemed like the top of heaven. Lush green hills carved by glaciers looked down on the fjord lands and deep blue ice hanging down into the waters. They were to spend one week in the Bergen Hotel. Though on the fourth night, they were woken by screaming and doors slamming. When Per opened his hotel room door, a drift of smoke choked the hallway.

"'Marda. Marda. Wake. Wake,' I yelled," is how Per told it. "I run to her and wake her. A beautiful woman. A sweet, round face. Big teeth. Her hair messed from sleep, and still beautiful. The far end of the hallway orange flame. A tunnel of fire crawling down the wood walls like a hungry dog. I shut door, and get wet towels for each of our faces. Should not have done that." It was here, every time he told the story, he paused. It was this decision, he clearly thought, that had ruined them.

"Marda was behind me when I open the door to hallway again. I pulled her forward but felt her fall back into the room. The heat scared her. We wait for minute in the room. We were children then. Scared. Should have acted quicker." He would speak of this as if it were what he did last night, the memory not dulled in the slightest by the seventy years which had since passed. He would repeat the same thing over and over. He talked slow, truly lucid only when telling this one story, the story of him and his first wife, half a world away, hunkered on the ledge of a burning fifth-floor hotel window.

"We held hands when it happened. When we jumped. I wished I'd hugged her as we went down. Held her in my arms." He would tear up a bit here, his recessed and runny eyes wetting more, glossing over.

Henry patted him on the knee.

"She landed, and then I landed on her, is how it went."

He stopped the story there.

If there were new people to listen, friends, or tourists who had taken the time to sit with the old man, Prissy could hear them at that moment. *Jesus. Dear Lord. Oh, no.* His silence, giving them the details they wanted most. Henry sat with him. He'd heard the story many times. But Prissy's grandfather had kept that part of his past a secret for decades, only unfurling it several years into the onset of dementia, only then letting it play over and over in a loop, sputtering out of him, making up for a lifetime of suppressing the want to tell people about how he'd jumped into the maw of a Norwegian night with the love of his life and landed alone.

In the other room Prissy copied the video onto fifty DVDs and prepared them with flyers to mail to a list of offices she got from a talent agency website.

After Prissy sent the disks, she started checking the mail as desperately as Sugar. At the mailbox each morning, still hoping for a letter from the patent office, Sugar would watch her.

He waved, "Anything?"

"Not yet," she said, blew him a kiss, and then walked back to the stables while thumbing through her mail, Lobo loping behind her. Just bills, she thought, as a yellow bi-plane piloted by a man who had looked down on the whole planet swooped overhead.

It was a month after sending the DVDs that Prissy received a letter from the Medieval Times dinner theatre in Rosemont, Illinois, outside of Chicago. *Dear Priscilla*, it read. *We would like to invite you to audition for a role in the upcoming year's troupe.* They had read articles about her in the local papers, *the woman who made horses swoon.* She could dress in frocks, stampede about a ring with clopping quarter horses and faux knights in armor made in China, and perform for Midwesterners eating turkey drumsticks with their hands, their children drinking root beers out of goblets.

"Wow. I really wanted my life to be bigger than this," she told Per.

"I should have held her as I jumped," he said.

She put a hand on her grandfather's knee. "I know, Papa."

Medieval Times would offer her enough money to pay for an apartment in the suburbs and cover the ranch's debt through the winter.

"Sugar would be able to watch out for you for a while," she told Per.

The Dancing Horses Show would wrap up for the season at the end of September. She'd have to be in Chicago by mid-October.

"It could be the change I need. It could be the start of something, Papa."

At the height of summer, Priscilla had a hard time sleeping on the very hot nights. She was tired when doing her morning chores. Slow-moving about the barn. From the rafter one morning, she gripped the steel railings, tossed her legs over the bars, and began sliding down as usual. But the cuff of her pants caught on a burr in the steel and her leg folded up and under her body as she slid. She felt a sharp popping in her right knee as the fabric caught and held her suspended upside-down from the ladder. Her screams brought Lobo who began barking and running in stupid circles. Lobo's barking brought Sugar who found Prissy inverted and weakly trying to right herself.

"My knee. My knee," she yelled as he picked her up and lifted her free.

Lobo kept barking as Sugar carried her from the barn to the truck. She couldn't stop crying on the drive to the ER at Olean General. Sugar watched as she explained to the receptionist that she didn't have an insurance card, and she was wheeled into the back room where they sat together and waited for two hours for the doctor to look at her.

A torn ACL. Surgery. A leg splint for months. Her summer of work at the Dancing Show and the potential exit to Rosemont, IL—gone. Rehab work. Scarring. Hidden scar tissue limiting future mobility. Weeks when she could only sit on the porch of her house, or in the barn, and watch Sugar and his father create nightmare hot rods for rich old men and their sons and grandsons. Several days of not getting out of bed. Her own down.

One night she opened her eyes and felt something was very wrong with her. A sudden madness. It was still dark. She managed to sit up but it was difficult to breathe. Her hands were shaking. Then she realized she couldn't move her leg at all. The outline of her things in the dark did not comfort her. She wanted to cry out but her chest was stopped up with an unnamed fear that had been on the periphery of her life for a long time but had now crested over, was seeping from her pores. She felt the hope she'd cradled for so long draining away. It felt like her body knew it too—was alerting her to it with this overwhelming panic.

At dawn, she woke to the sounds of Lobo vomiting in the yard. A cool blue breath slipped in through the window, and the crisp cloak of morning drew her deeper beneath the covers. The vividness of what would never happen in her life formed a solid ache in the center of her chest.

That night, Sugar looked up a Thomas J. Kelly in the local phonebook. He found the address on the Avenue of Champions in the golf course. After it got dark, he snuck out of the trailer and biked to the golf course with his potato launching gun slung by a canvas strap around his back. The budding tassels of the corn stalks swayed in the breeze. Fireflies burned a quick glowing green over the soy fields. He biked past horse pastures and up the country road to the back entrance of the Art Instituion where they didn't keep a guard at the gate after ten. When the headlights of a car came up the road behind him he biked off the side and lay down in the pine trees.

When the car passed, he biked on, into the maze of roads and subdivisions until he found Hurst Avenue and worked his way along the numbered mailboxes to 147, the Kelly address, a standalone home with a three-car garage and the Shelby Mustang Sugar had just sold parked in the driveway.

Leaving his bike in a crop of bushes he snuck through the woods lining a fairway with his potato launching gun. His range was about a hundred feet which he could hit from the woods. What he really wanted was to destroy the car, to pull it apart panel by panel and leave the rivets scattered on the driveway. He dug in the woods for a rock the size of a baseball. When he found one, he lined up the PVC pipe nozzle and aimed high into the air so the rock would arch upward and smash on top of the car. The detailed paint job gave him a moment of hesitation, but it was no longer his, it had been sold to some stranger who had more than he would ever have. The ensuing flash of anger led him to pull the trigger. The rock launched high into the darkness where he saw the gray shape of it disappear and then there was only the sound of the seventeen year cicada's insane racket, broken by a large smashing sound of the rock cracking and shattering the windshield.

He loaded in another rock, aimed it and fired. When that rock left a deep dent on the hood, he ran back to his bike. There were no cars on the country road as he returned home.

After her third day of not getting out of bed, Sugar marched into the house in the evening, drew a bath, lifted Prissy from the bed, and delivered her, fully dressed, into the water.

"What the hell?" she yelled.

He said nothing. He had a giant horse sponge. New. Still in the wrapper. He opened it in the water, then peeled back her sopping shirt, the tan fabric of her bra now a deep, wet brown. He picked up the sponge, squeezed it under the water, and ran it over her neck and shoulders.

"I can manage," she said, swatting him away, but he kept rubbing and she stopped fighting. She shut her eyes and let his thick, hard hands run heavy between her shoulder blades, over the bra strap which he undid, and keep rubbing. Generations of men with hands like these led to these mitts. It was not different from wild bloodlines in horses. She eased back as Sugar stripped her naked, and washed her until the water ran cold. Then he lifted her out, wrapped her tight in a loose bed sheet and carried her to the porch where she could feel the evening breeze on her cocooned body. He said nothing the whole time. Neither did she.

"What can I get you to dress in?" he asked. He was being sweet. She resented him for it. She wanted to be left alone. She wanted to be mean.

"Look at yourself," she said. She eyed the markings of deep blue India Ink beneath his skin. "You're a joke. You look like a bad cartoon of a male stripper. It's a goddamn sad mess."

"You trying to cut me deep now or something?" Sugar said, tucking a tuft of hair behind his ear

"Yeah, you wouldn't even know."

"Don't pretend like you know enough about me."

"What's to pretend? I do know everything about you." She looked out past him toward the open field. The budding tassels of the corn stalks swayed in the breeze. "You'll be here forever. I'll lose my fucking mind if I have to stay here forever. You know that. You know it, but you do all this shit to make me stay. You want me to stay and be your little sex pet across the street. You want to own me."

He kept standing beside her, willing to take whatever came at him.

"I don't want to be stuck here forever," she buried her face into the sheet. "You have no idea how bad I want to work my way out of here. I mean, why this place for our lives? Do the other people who live here have these problems?"

The sky was darkening, with big, pastel clouds drifting past. A soft breeze rustled the branches.

"What can I get you to wear?" Sugar asked again.

She looked at him, at his face, and those eyes that were the same as long as she'd known him, Sugar's eyes, Samuel Bergman's eyes, the little boy; the same ones that had seen so much of her.

"There's a purple shirt on a hanger in the right of my closet," she said. It was her best shirt. The one with the scooped neck that showed her breasts off when she didn't wear a bra. It felt like the one to wear now. "And a pair of jean shorts in a stack above that." Those showed off her legs, even with the scars, made it clear she was still something to look at. He went back into the house to get the clothes and came back out with them from around the side, where he climbed out of her bedroom window from years of habit.

"Typical," she said, and let out a short laugh which made him aware of what he'd done, and he smiled at her. Then he gave her the clothes and helped her get dressed right on the porch. There were times she had looked at him and thought he was some sort of sick cockroach man with his yellowed tan, beefed-up muscles, and ink tucked under his skin. But now, his fingers reached through the filthy gray accumulation of years, culling the memory of nights they had spent together without ever getting dressed. He pulled her up against him. The rough, dry pads of his fingertips snapped on the elastic of her blue lace panties. The ensuing electric jolt across her body surprised her. If a tourist drove by at that moment, they'd see the horses, the saddled team waiting for them, and what looked like a giant male stripper dressing a naked horse acrobat in the last of the daylight.

As Sugar dressed Prissy, he felt like he had now been given his real life. Prissy would stay. Well, probably stay. She may regret part of it, but he could give her everything in him now. He could unlock what was held back and offer it all over. It all seemed so grand, random, and out of his control. He sat next to her on the porch and looked over the horse fields to his barn.

Near dark the Shelby Mustang with a spider-webbed windshield and ruined hood pulled onto the road and into his driveway. Thomas J. Kelly stepped out and looked around.

Sugar stood up. "Over here Mr. Kelly."

Thomas J. Kelly waved to Sugar. "I was hoping to pay you to do some repairs for me."

"Sure thing," Sugar yelled, and he stood up and made to cross the road to where he built chrome-plated machines that could carry him away at two hundred miles an hour.

"I'll be back," he told Prissy who tamed half-ton animals and made them dance in cones of white light.

As he walked, he sensed the power the two of them held was child's play; it would forever be dwarfed by a past that was always burning forward, dripping from the mouth of Per, carried along by Iroquois names, or swooping back in tightly-scrolled notes on the gnarled legs of homing pigeons, anchoring them, ever-growing children, to their place on the earth and scorching through one life to the next.

LEVI'S RECESSION

Spring:

During training they tell you the first thing to do in case of an emergency is go back into the trailer and upright the animals so they don't crush each other. But after the accident the truck was on its side and I'd fallen across the cab and crashed headfirst into the passenger door. When I stood up my feet were where the window had been, my chin was even with the steering wheel, and the air tasted like aluminum and hog piss. Before stepping into the sleeping compartment I thought the awful sound in the cab was some side-effect of a ruptured eardrum singing out deep in my head. A pile of blankets, pillows, whittling blocks for carving, and DVDs were at my feet as I put my ear against the metal wall and listened to the terrible squealing of what had been seventy-five full-grown pigs.

I pulled myself up onto the cab's side panel through the driver's window. Trees lined the fields on either side of me. A menacing blue-gray cloud bank stacked up on the horizon and sharpened in color as it approached. The cab had scraped its way over eighty feet of the road after jackknifing and the line of gouges in the asphalt left by the trailer ended at me.

I'd been driving fast—too fast. My shoulder and head hurt and I was lucky not to have been killed. I leapt down off the cab and walked along the truck's undercarriage. It was hard getting the trailer's back gate open, and when it fell loose it hit the street hard and just missed taking off my toes. Five pigs ran past me and started milling around on the side of the road. The individual gates penning the hogs in swung open like a wall of steel mouths. I stepped in and walked the length of the trailer as the pigs' squealing chorus gathered and swelled around me.

None of them were dead. A few were stuck on their sides. Several more had hoofs sticking through the grates, and one that somehow had a leg sticking out the vent the trailer had fallen and slid on was bleeding from a pulpy stump hanging off its shoulder. I went into that one's pen and did the only thing I could think of to help it. I straddled it, pulled my serrated pocket knife from the worn leather sheaf on my belt, and plunged the point in under its jaw, slicing it across its carotid artery which was tough at first, then gave easy like a padded couch as I tore the blade up and to the side.

Maybe I wasn't thinking after that, or maybe it was that amber light inside of me beginning to fade into an overpowering need to do something, but I began herding the rest of the hogs out of the trailer by slapping them on their meaty haunches.

By the time the police showed up all the pigs were wandering around in the field and no one was going to catch any of them. It was shocking how fast they could move, and, after a couple of attempts, the police decided they didn't know what to do with them if they were caught since the trailer was still on its side, so they were let free to graze on the recently-thawed cornstalks sticking out of the snow. The hogs ate their way to the line of trees and then wandered off into the woods toward the Allegheny River.

The company man who the police contacted was supportive when I first talked to him from the crash site. He was all, "I'm glad you're okay, Levi," and "You did the best you could, Levi." Then he found out I was five miles from my ex-wife's house, which had been my destination, and about forty miles east of Interstate 90, where I should've been, when I lost control on the ice.

"There's a problem with my daughter," I said.

"I see," he said.

"It's an emergency," I said, but that didn't mean anything to him and as soon as we hung up he was on the phone to the company lawyers to see how fast they could fire me. That's what they did too. "We're going to have to let you go, Levi," he told me later, which was about the worst thing that could've happened. I was making good money that I needed driving those pigs.

I didn't want to go to the hospital, so a tall and ropey state trooper named Terry drove me from the crash site to my ex-wife's house. Merriam's old farm house is on the high ground outside of Olean. As the trooper drove, my gaze glided over the fields beside the road, white with the last hard snow pushing down the husks of alfalfa and rye. A coolness seeped into me as the squad car rattled down one back road after another. I wanted to get to Merriam's as fast as possible and yet never get there, never find out what news was waiting.

That morning Merriam called me on the road to tell me our twenty-year-old daughter, Nedra, had been missing for over a week. As the trooper drove, terrible things that could have happened played on a loop in my head. When Nedra was sixteen she got herself an ambulance ride to Olean General Hospital where they discovered she'd smashed Xanax in with what must have been a titanic line of cocaine. What she had gotten into before that I couldn't begin to guess, but since then, she'd moved on to finding darker and stranger ways to cause herself harm. There was a spell where I'd scream like a lunatic at her and her mother would guilt her up and down and cry in front of her, but none of that worked. I'd look at her skinny, pale legs, her dust-green eyes, and the narrow draw of her face she'd gotten from me and my heart would lurch against my ribs because she seemed to be throwing her life away.

A mile before Merriam's house the road turns from pavement to gravel. The ticking of the stones striking the bottom of the car used to be a welcoming sound to me and they snapped my focus to the curve of the driveway leading up to the old farm house. When the trooper pulled up to the house Merriam was on the porch waiting with my best friend, Mick. She saw the police car and started running towards it. When she saw it was me getting out, her face slackened in immediate disappointment.

Merriam is slight as a heron and the crown of her head lines up with my chin. Her pale ivory pallor is covered in shadowy brown freckles that fade into one another and make torn leaf-shaped splotches that I've traced with my fingernail. Her red hair changes shades three times on its endless descent over her back and is a fiery burnt umber where the ends brush against her hamstrings.

"I thought they'd found her," she said. "Jesus, I don't know what we're going to do," her voice quivered like she'd had the air forced out of her.

"Is there something you need help with, ma'am?" Terry asked.

"We don't want her to get a record," I whispered as she leaned against my chest.

"But what if…"

"We're not there yet," I said.

"No. We're okay for now, officer," she said.

"Thatta girl," I said, getting the first scent of her lavender shampoo that I'd had in a long time. I shut my eyes for a moment and held her with that very real feeling of still loving her creeping up from my fingertips.

When I opened my eyes again Mick was standing next to us.

"We'll find her," he said.

He had on his Carhartts with the threadbare holes in the knees. He wore a grease-stained blue and gold Buffalo Sabres cap with the bill curved tight over his temples like a claw. "Where's your truck?" Merriam asked, and all the facts of my life pushed the scent of lavender away. All those problems with our daughter, and the inevitable hurts that got caked on us as we went along, poured back.

"I'll tell you later," I said. The trooper's car was crunching the gravel behind me as it pulled out of the driveway and the sound made her chest sink further inside her body.

"We'll find her," Mick said. And he pointed to his truck. "I'll fill you in as we go."

I followed him to the truck and got in.

We drove Mick's '85 Ford till late at night when exhaustion from the last of the morning adrenaline rush faded and I felt numb for hours until the first birds of the new day were trilling and there was Mick hunched over the wheel still driving. His sweaty aftershave smell filled the cab. His eyes were pinned on the road ahead of him. He had a high forehead and stubby nose, but broad shoulders and the lean torso of a scavenger bird. His large meaty hands rested on the steering wheel and his callused fingers kept tapping in rhythm on the dashboard. He came from Scandinavian stock that adjusted to life in the Allegheny foothills and he was hardened by humorless immigrant parents who squashed any dreams he may have had when he was young of living an alternate life. He was as much a part of this place as the trees and he knew every last corner to search.

"We'll find her," Mick said. "She's a bit wild is all. Like her Daddy used to be."

Mick and I had gone to high school together, and though we had never been great friends when we were younger, we seemed to be each other's only friends as we approached middle age.

We spent two days together searching for Nedra along a hundred-and-thirty-mile stretch of the Southern Tier Highway winding east from Lake Erie, following the river into the flat fields, up into the foothills, from Chautauqua Institution to Olean, the Seneca Indian Reservation, and Allegany State Park. If I hadn't been so scared I'd have thought there was nothing prettier than that big curved windshield facing the first of the day's sun and then the last tendrils of pastel leeching from the sky. Between those tricks of sunlight were the endless hash-marks on back roads, rise after rise of rolling hills until we dropped west into the prairie land beat down by green and yellow harvest combines and chemical trucks with large plastic tanks and long metal booms, and lonely ramshackle barns with wood slats sliced by razors of light and overrun with clumps of brush that dotted the horizon.

We checked the closed-down city pool, the Olean library, Whetstone Knife factory, the hockey rink, The Dancing Horses show theatre, the ski hill, cider mill, the combination gas station and deli Nedra and her friends used to play in the snow mountains as kids, and even the Amish settlement where they have the puppy mill, a barn full of Newfoundlands, golden retrievers, and poodles they breed for pet stores. We kept driving past the hospital, nursing home, a rural airfield with a lone yellow bi-plane in the grass next to the runway, and an old railroad strip where Teddy Roosevelt once stumped from the back of a train car.

How big this one small place was, and how full, filled me with anxiety that I would not be able to find Nedra. I hoped someone, somewhere, sometime, would take care of my girl.

For a moment I imagined I were the Canadian missionary, the first westerner who founded the area. How he discovered the first oil deposit on North America in nearby Cuba. How that discovery later led to the Allegheny River Valley being one of the richest fossil fuel depositories on earth. That man must have stumbled into this land.

We stopped for gas and coffee. There was a McDonald's, a Dairy Queen, and Circle K gas station off the exit. This exit looked like every other highway exit in the country. At the Circle K gas station several eighteen wheelers filled up at the pumps and a row of about ten more rigs idled in the back lot. There, men slept in their cabs. Watched movies. I've spent half a lifetime with men like them and knew I could take a .38 special from cab to cab, force confessions, and uncover any number of terrible crimes. I wanted to do that. To hold up a picture of my girl. Demand a path to find her.

I went inside to ask everyone if they'd seen her. Mick was still in the bathroom. There was a trucker's lounge with a television and coin laundry station that was in use. Fox News was on. I tried to listen but all I ever hear is everyone thinks everyone else is stupid. I looked for a map. The only thing they had to read were three different gun and hunting magazines, two car magazines with girls in G-strings sprawled over the hoods, and a breakdown of the Buffalo Bills roster with picture inserts of all the players.

"I've got all those at home. You don't need to buy anything here," Mick said.

"I'd like a map," I told him.

"Won't help."

"Why not?"

He pointed over the top of the trucks. "You see those hillsides. Well, you slip down the backside of any of these hills and you'll find a dirt road not on any map. It will take you to some home you'd be surprised to find there. These hills stretch over two thousand miles clear down to Georgia. You know that. No map will tell us that. We've just got to keep looking."

We left and headed south. A rehabbed Cadillac Fleetwood with a V16 turned off a new development road onto the opposite lane and Mick waved for it to slow down. When Mick rolled the window down he knocked the lid of his coffee loose and it sloshed down his chest.

"Dammit."

He pulled the cloth away from his skin and let it slap back down a few times.

"You seen a young woman with brown hair and a round face running around here?" he yelled out the window to the car stopped next to us. A clean cut old man with a giant golden retriever in the passenger seat shook his head no, nodded goodbye, and kept on driving.

Off I-86 there was a small white chapel with a stained glass window framed above the wide wooden doors. The window was blue at the base with a brown-robed Jesus walking on water, a yellow light flooding the panes over his head.

"I hope I'm not to the point I need to start praying," I told Mick.

He studied the church and the bright glass as we passed. "Not yet."

We made our way to The Tavern, a dive bar in Olean. Out front there was a truck towing a 1920 Packard Twin Six on a flatbed trailer. Kelly Gynobly, the bartender, was a large woman with short black hair who always wore tank top shirts that showed her muscular shoulders and bare neckline. Kelly also had a red mucus sack held in by a sheen of silver skin instead of a right eyeball. The sack sunk beneath the ledge of her eye socket like a large larva egg. Her younger brother hit the eye dead-on with a pellet launched from a slingshot when they were kids and that did something akin to turning the eyeball inside out. The globe swallowed the pellet and held it like a pearl.

"Kelly, darling. Can you come down here a minute?" Mick said.

"Excuse me," she said to the tan man at the end of the bar. Though he now had a blond ponytail and tattoos and looked nothing like he used to, I recognized him as Samuel Bergman from my old high school days.

"You doin okay, hun?" she asks Mick.

"What's Samuel up to over there?" I lean in.

"Samuel? You mean Sugar? He's collecting old cars again."

I look at "Sugar," his fake yellowed tan and broad shoulders, the barbwire tattoo around his muscular arm. Could he be the man who took my girl?

"We're looking for Nedra," Mick said, jolting me back to attention.

"Haven't seen her in a few nights," Kelly said.

"She's been here though?" I asked.

"She's here all the time," Kelly said, her eye falling away from me.

"She's only twenty," I said.

"No different than when it was our turn at sneaking in here."

I wanted to knock the little stack of tomato juice cans off the bar, pull her towards me and shake her until she told me where Nedra was.

"Kelly," Mick said. "She's been gone for a week now and we need to find her."

Kelly tugged the white bar rag taut between her hands. "She was in here three nights ago."

"Who was she with?" Mick asked.

"Didn't know the person."

My guts sank when she said that from having listened to police scanners for years while driving, overhearing the chatter of so many small, terrible crimes.

"What'd he look like?" Mick asked.

"Not sure to be honest. Not sure where she went to after leaving either. I'm sorry guys. I wish there was more to tell you."

After leaving The Tavern we kept along the Allegheny River. We drove for several hours through Olean, Jamestown, and Dunkirk on winding back roads that didn't have names. Halfway down County Road H the news channel fuzzed out, overlaid by a baritone preacher out of eastern Ohio. We passed through small towns and stopped into dairy farmers' homes that we knew and asked our questions. On the deeply-rutted Quaker Run Road in Allegany State Park along the river we saw the tent through the trees. It was the two-person, winterized, yellow pop tent that Merriam bought for Nedra years earlier. When Nedra was a girl I would set that tent up in our backyard and we'd sleep outside in it on warm summer nights and use flashlights to cast finger shadows on the nylon walls. Mick and I got out of the truck and marched through the woods up to the tent. I unzipped the flap, pulled it back, and my heart started lurching again.

There was my daughter, tangled up in the arms and legs of some skinny little woman who was kissing her collarbone. They shot up and started rocking on their sleeping bags, each hyper as hell.

"Get away," the woman yelled. Her voice pierced the quiet of the woods.

A yeasty, caustic sex smell, something chemical on top of something base and very human, floated past me and made my eyes water.

I guess I knew then what was making them so jumpy. Next to their flattened pillow were wads of tinfoil and a light bulb blackened by the purple Bic lighter in the corner of the tent.

"What have you done?" I gasped.

The woman with Nedra was topless and had small breasts with nickel-sized, salmon-colored nipples. A thin cord of blue veins threaded across her forearms and disappeared into her wrists. Her thin auburn hair was disheveled and there were deep circles under her eyes that looked like torn walnut husks. A twitch on her cheek kept pulling up her lip exposing her gum line. She put a hand on my daughter's leg and squeezed her pants in her fist like she was trying to keep me from taking her away.

Nedra gave me this half-crazed look and I knew she'd been smoking meth, too. She focused her stare over my shoulder and looked at Mick with this strange gravity and swatted the topless woman's hand away from her leg without breaking eye contact with him.

"Did you miss me?" she said looking past me and the last of her words were bitten off by something dark and mean.

I pulled Nedra out of the tent by her arm. "What have you done?" I repeated. Her eyes, which turned to me for a moment, jumped back to Mick.

"What the hell are you looking at?" I yelled. "What's going on?"

There was a history in her stare. I felt it. It started burning up my spine and I wanted to hammer my fists into all three of them.

Mick looked at me and shook his head and kicked at sprigs of dead grass and snow-covered dirt at his feet.

Nedra was trying to wiggle loose but I clamped on tighter and began pulling her to the truck. My fingers wrapped around her upper arm tight enough to leave a bruise. I wanted to leave a bruise.

"What do we do with that one?" Mick said, pointing to the other woman.

"Leave her," I said. "She found her way out here, she'll get back."

Hearing that, the woman stood and stepped out of the tent. Despite the small bags under her eyes and the full heft of her near-nakedness she looked like a child, desperate and vulnerable in this nowhere and alone place.

Nedra kept pulling against my grip which didn't break and then waved the woman over.

"Put some clothes on, at least," Mick said. Something in his voice sounded disgusted.

The woman sat in the flatbed of the truck as we drove back to The Tavern. I have to say I'm glad we didn't leave her in the woods. It wouldn't have sat well with me if we had.

At The Tavern, Sugar's truck with the Packard had moved on. Kelly came outside and walked to our truck before the engine turned off. It was the only time I'd ever seen her in daylight outside of the bar and her bad eye looked like a rotting cherry reflecting a wrinkle of light. She helped the freezing cold woman out of the truck and wrapped her own jacket around her.

"It's okay, Donna," Kelly said.

"You know her?" I asked.

Kelly didn't look back at me but blew a kiss to my daughter and led the woman into the bar. It was one of those touching and tragic things you end up seeing over the course of a life.

Nedra had little scabs up and down her arms like a severe case of chicken pox that she dug at in the truck between me and Mick as we drove. She homed in on one spot and dug and dug her fingers in until there it was, there was my own blood coming out of this skinny little thing. An overpowering wave of affection towards her washed through me—that original softness that first came to me when she was born, when it was clear how helpless she was.

By the time the small stones on Merriam's road started smacking the undercarriage of the truck, Nedra began coming unglued between us. Her body went slack as a bag of water and she slouched forward with the crown of her head facing her lap. Then she shot up, her spine stiff, and rocked side to side between us, pressing into my shoulder and then away. Her hairline was beaded with sweat, her eyes jittered around in her head, and there was very little I recognized in this thin, strange creature.

"We're going to fall through the road," she said. Her voice was slow, soft, muffled by layers of spider webs at the back of her throat. Then her head rolled against the seat as she arched her rubber spine backwards.

Dear God. I used to play I-Spy with her when we drove, and now this.

"All the way down," was the last thing she mumbled before Merriam ran out and led her out of the truck and into the house, where we forced her into a freezing bath and my daughter spent the night swinging from paranoid to euphoric, back and forth as if she were on the very edge of life.

That first night after we'd found Nedra was spent talking to doctors, and then on their advice, figuring out how to pay for the rehab clinic near the Chautauqua Institution Mick let me stay with him after the loss of my trucking job, and I did for a few days after Merriam and I dropped Nedra off at the clinic. He lived by himself outside of town, along the Allegheny River. He started a drywall company after high school and kept the garage attached to this house full of tools, sheetrock, and his flat-hulled aluminum fan boat and its trailer. Dust from the garage clung to Blutcher, his Newfoundland dog, who licked his dreadlocked ass all day long, lapping his fur up into a nauseating froth that gave him shit breath when he came to put his head on your lap.

"You've got to give this mutt a bath," I said.

"He swims in the river," Mick said.

Blutcher had a worn-down dog bed in the living room of Mick's small house but followed Mick from room to room and lay at his feet.

The dingy dining room had old wood veneer wall paneling and no furniture, but there were half a dozen sawhorses where he worked indoors through the winter. The floorboards were caked in drywall dust and the scent of creosote filled the air. A three-tiered tackle box lay open in the corner and the scatter of tools inside gave the room an industrial, lonely feeling. Carpenter rulers and levels were strewn about as if he had a constant need to do something measured, to weigh an accomplishment to give each day its worth. Blutcher swatted at a screwdriver and gnawed on a splintered corner of a board and I envied the company of his dog who must have helped stem off the pain of total solitude.

After a few days at Mick's, a mounting unease about not working ballooned beneath my ribs and the way he had stared back at Nedra in the tent kept moving through my head. Little flashes of her on her back in the bed of his truck or on some old dog blanket with the bottom of her feet facing straight up led to my fantasizing about crashing a claw hammer into his head.

"Mick," I said, "I've got something to ask you."

He turned toward me. The knots of muscles at the top of his jaw line tensed and leaned into me like he wanted me to slug him.

"Go ahead."

And I did want to hit him, to unburden myself, but something in the way he offered himself up and the sad surroundings of his undecorated home made me change my mind. I also was sure Blutcher would tear my arm off if I lifted it against Mick. It wasn't the right time to know what had happened with him and my daughter as knowing meant losing him too. But I couldn't stay there any longer.

Merriam had an old Airstream trailer behind her house. Inside there was a sheath of dust on the window ledges and countertops but it was comfortable. Beyond the trailer on her property was a dense thicket of pine trees where her grandfather planted a Christmas tree farm with the notion of selling them over the holidays. That was before he ran off with another woman, leaving the trees to become a perfectly-ordered forest only sixty years later.

"I don't want to be in your hair anymore so I'll move into the trailer behind Merriam's house," I said, and something in his face slackened and released. We were quiet then, pinned to each other by the sharp corners of what needed to be said but wasn't.

Summer:

At the end of May, the rivers in Cattaraugus County flooded. The Allegheny rose so high over its banks the fields three miles on either side turned into small lakes. Rows of corn stalks rose out of the dark waters and the soybean fields were covered outright. In the valleys, islands of elm trees floated across the horizon next to old, ranch-style farmhouses. In town, water filled the basements and root cellars and pushed away the cinder blocks propping up old cars so that the vehicles slumped into the rising murk.

The grass that stood so straight and swayed with the slightest breeze was now flat to the ground, and when the water level dropped, it angled towards the receding flood waters as if each blade were reaching, thirsty for more. Whole fields and forests swirled into mesmerizing mud pits and prowling swampland.

When people came out to see the damage, it was with slack, silent faces. They lifted up waterlogged clothing and shook it out one or two times as if that would dry it off. Then they dropped everything they'd picked up back into the slop at their feet, realizing it couldn't be salvaged.

Within days of the water receding, the front lawns were piled with soggy carpets and drywall torn off the struts with the tips of glittering nails sticking out in every direction. Each home had a pile in front of it that started as a few rotten boards, then grew into a pulpy mass made from the contents of the home.

Some people in town had flood insurance, and those on the outside of town that probably didn't seemed too embarrassed to say anything either way. People either took comfort in the fact that things could be repaired, or sank knowing that this was going to leave its watermark on the rest of their lives.

The liquor store Merriam worked at was ruined. The bottles with the warped labels and the soaked boxes got counted as destroyed and a check from some large insurance company would come for the purposes of restocking the store. But the bottle seals weren't compromised, so Kevin, the shop's owner, let Mick and I take what we wanted home with us. We took seven full loads in Mick's Ford and pulled the air boat from his garage, loading the empty space with the cases. When that was full, we moved onto Merriam's basement, which was up on the town's bluff and still dry, and filled it wall to wall with flood-damaged liquor—enough that we could drink until our skin turned a different color. When the room was full, boxes rose up in stacks that left a narrow walkway to move through and the room smelled musty from the wet cardboard.

Mick hired me on to start clearing out some of the nicer homes in the surrounding towns. People were paying cash to have the most immediate work done before the insurance checks came in. We worked around the clock for almost a month, cutting loose the soggy drywall and lumber where it was going to cause mold damage. We also gutted and replastered an outbuilding on the Whetstone property. I ended up sleeping at Mick's again so we could roll out of bed to get right to work. When we came home Blutcher would tear out in a fury to chase after the truck and bite at his reflection in the hubcaps, getting washed in the dust and gravel kicked up by the tires.

"At least he knows how ugly he is," Mick said, as he parked next to the fan boat.

After the official insurance claims were filed, tradesmen paid by some big insurance company came from Buffalo, Cleveland, Pittsburgh, and anywhere else they could be contracted to make the drive, and work for us dried up.

After more than a month of her being in rehab, we were allowed to see Nedra. Merriam and I got in a fight on the start of our drive to Chautauqua and we drove the rest of the way with silent accusations and anger brewing between us. Those little fights had sapped me. That was why I liked being alone on the road all those years. Being *married* to my wife was enough for me; it quelled the manic need to fill my heart that consumed most of my youth. But being with the woman, under the same roof, drained me of something that felt essential. That was my deepest confession and at the heart of why my marriage failed. It may well lie at the heart of why my daughter was seeking her own self-destruction.

At the clinic Nedra was led into a visiting room where the two of us were. She wore pajamas and her hair was long and greasy like she hadn't washed it in weeks. She stood on the other end of the room from us and didn't say a word, didn't move, and it was a horrifying moment where none of us knew what to do. Then she stepped forward with her shoulders and arms still slack at her side and walked into her mother's chest to be hugged. She buried her head in the nape of Merriam's neck and didn't look at me. And maybe it was because she didn't look at me that I was pierced again with another of those little grappling hooks, those fine strings that Nedra flung at my heart to suspend herself by. I felt the weight of her hanging at the center of my life, a spectacular marionette attached by millions of glowing strings like a cascading harp. She swayed back and forth, a pendulum pushing aside who I had been until she consumed everything else that ever mattered to me.

"I want to go home," she said.

Merriam and I had spent our negative energy on that drive to Nedra, and after we brought her home it was easier to be together. We both felt the pull to linger around the house and watch over our girl. We got in the habit at night of sitting on the porch together and looking out at the dark wall of giant swaying Christmas trees. It was nice sitting with her and it helped me forget about the weight of panic that made me feel small in a way I feared I couldn't recover from.

When it was clear Mick and I weren't going to get any more local work, and the liquor store was closed until it could be renovated, Merriam and I decided to tap into our new liquor supply. We brought a lunch cooler of ice outside to fill our cups with and listen to the seventeen year cicadas. Merriam drank vanilla-flavored vodka, and I drank a fifteen-year-old scotch that had the labels soaked off.

The glue beaded up on the bottle and I scraped what was left of it off with my thumbnail. Some nights Mick would come over and Nedra would even sit out with us, brooding as she sipped on a fruity iced tea, speaking in choppy, regurgitated therapy-speak.

"I'm feeling pretty down tonight." She even worked in a bit of melodrama, saying things like, "I need to work on my self-worth."

What I wanted was for her to come out and tell me what she needed, so I listened, asking her to keep talking when her words trailed off so she might unburden all her secrets we had yet to discover. But she was still jumpy; the meth had changed the chemistry of her brain. She shifted herky-jerky-like, as if her bones were trying to wiggle out of her dry, flushed skin. I drank my scotch, letting the peat flavor swell on the back of my tongue and watched her, equally happy she was safe and home and furious with the monster of her own wasted promise.

On a night Mick didn't come over and Nedra didn't get out of bed, Merriam suggested we drive my truck across the field to the river. We brought drinks and a blanket. When we got there we slowly got drunk while sitting on the tailgate of my truck. Then she leaned in and started kissing me. That led to us going at it in my truck, wildly tearing at each other, as it had been so long since we'd even touched. Flashes of her body filled the dark—a rounded curve of her bare calf muscle, her breast falling away from her rib cage beneath swaths of her wild orange hair. She had long pubic hair, something she had always trimmed down when we were married. I grabbed it between my fingers and pulled till it was taut and then give it a yank to push her over the edge. It was as if we were strangers and this didn't come with all the weight of our previous lives—divorce, misspent time, things ruined, people hurt—which had always flooded back so damn quick and stayed for so long that it felt like a miracle for us to be able to be near each other now. This pretending we had no such past, even for a moment, felt like it was saving us.

She lay belly down on the flatbed of the truck. Her hair draped over the exposed knobs of her spine and fanned out to cover the nape of her pink back. I put my palms on each of her butt cheeks and rubbed in concentric circles until she clenched up, began to laugh and rolled over and pulled me next to her so we were lying stomach to stomach and looking into each other's faces.

After a while, perhaps so we wouldn't have to talk, she said she wanted to fire my gun. I turned the headlights on and we stood in front of the truck to shoot. My first shot popped off and the long echo of the single chamber deer rifle thrummed over us. When it was her turn to fire I stepped back to see the smooth lines of her naked body as she aimed my rifle into the woods. Her skin glowed in the headlights. She fired. The recall kicked hard and the rifle fell from her hands. When she turned towards me there was a one-inch crescent moon gash on her forehead from the gun's scope snapping back. The mark welled up and blood flowed over her eyes and down both sides of her nose before dripping onto her bare chest. She fell to her hands and knees and threw her hair over her head. I reached for something from our pile of clothes to clot the blood with and came away with my sock which I pressed against her head until the bleeding stopped. Then I used the other sock to clean her off but smeared blood across her body.

After bandaging the cut on her head back at the house, she went to bed. I went to the stoop of the trailer to try to sober up and think about what to do and tried to convince myself it was okay to be idle for a while, but even the idea made me uneasy. I thought about everywhere I'd been while driving trucks to calm myself down.

If I traced my driving career, I'd dig the pen into a large circle around Interstate 90 and scratch it in until the paper tore and there was a big hole in the map of the country—like those years had indeed, as Nedra put it, fallen through the road. Interrupted by rest stops, Country Inn Suites, and Cracker Barrels, my years were measured in miles and passed in the dark, moving hogs and cows around the middle of the country, stopping in those nowhere railroad towns out west in Nebraska: Red Cloud, Oxbow, and even near Kearny during the sandhill crane migrations, when millions of birds bottlenecked over that twenty-mile stretch of highway and filled the sky. At the big truck stops, I power-hosed out the animal shit and scrubbed the floors and walls. I did stretches on the truck, leaning against the cab and doing dips from the foot ladder and pull-ups hanging off the trailer with my legs kicked under it. There was very little spectacular about the whole thing, but I missed seeing strangers lugging U-Hauls and going about the business of changing their lives, and I missed the perpetual motion of having somewhere to be, having some task that needed doing.

I wasn't going to get another job driving a rig anytime soon, so I looked for work as a technician working on the giant windmills springing up all over, but would have had to go back to school at the community college to get certified. So most of that first part of summer I floundered, playing house cop to my daughter and making sure she didn't sneak off anywhere else. I'd look in on her every night, then sit on the deck of my trailer and stare at the woods. That's how I discovered the shadow that stalked our property in the dark.

First, there was a flicker of dark black off in the distance that my eyes shot to. Then the shadow moved again, growing as it got closer. When it moved a third time it became clear those swinging arms and distinct gait belonged to a grown man. I was about to ease over and grab my rifle from the truck when the blue brim of a Sabres cap caught a sliver of moonlight in the field. Mick moved from tree to tree and then stopped to look at our house. He must not have seen me as he walked out of the woods and started taking long, slow steps to the back of the house where Nedra's bedroom window was. In the open the full outline of his body took shape: thick shoulders; the beginning of a padded mid-section; slightly-bowed, long legs; and always the curved brim of that blue cap.

Mick kept walking closer and closer in those slow, methodical steps. Part of me wanted to see how close he'd dare get but when the premonition he'd actually peer through the glass hit me, I made a throat-clearing sound. He froze in mid-stride and his silhouette lingered at this odd angle like some ugly sculpture. Then he turned back and with the same slow steps began his retreat to the woods.

After that night I often caught a glimpse of my only friend lurking behind tree trunks in the shadows. How long the habit had been going on I had no idea. I tried to convince myself he was watching over my family, warding off whatever unlucky spirit had crashed into our house, but I knew better—I knew he was part of the messy rut our lives were stuck in.

I had a hundred chances to confront Mick about what he was doing at my daughter's window but every time I thought of doing something a deep sadness filled me that kept me from saying a word. Before I knew it, it was late summer, and we were spending time together working on his air boat, checking the hull and aluminum prow for dents or cracks that needed to be pounded out, welded, or patched. We took off the fan cover and wiped the caked layer of smashed bugs off each blade, then we checked the motor, ratcheting the gears tighter and flushing out the silt and shards of olive grass.

When it was ready we trucked it on Mick's trailer and backed it into the water so we could start exploring the river for the night.

On the Allegheny's widest and longest straightaway, still deep from the floods, Mick opened up the throttle on his fan boat. The motor vibrated up the chair through my legs and the fan felt like it was going to suck me backwards if I didn't hold on.

He lit a Coleman camping lantern and the fiery mesh bag burned an orange ring that rose up towards the fixture where it exploded into painful white light that whistled the rest of the night until the propane ran out. We bolted it onto the bow and the light gave us ten feet of visibility as we glided downstream like some amped-up waterfowl over the vile murk of the river.

The skeleton of a rusted old car was sunk into the riverbank. The chassis was packed into the mud but the petrified engine block was exposed. It was now one rust-fused heap of steel. Flecks of rust chipped from the body drifted downriver, glittering orange and fine as sand. In the slime-rimmed shallows near the car, bullfrogs groaned to each other as they ate up the bug larvae floating in the stagnant eddies. Downriver there was a sandbank with white egrets roosting for the night. When we fired the engine up and started blowing towards them they shook their bodies loose and lifted off the water and spread out against the manic scatter of stars. Smaller birds darted across the water for insects. An owl fluttered past like a ripple in the dark. Night hunters were about the business of looking, and always looking for something—that longing—felt natural to me too, as if I were wired to search for the missing part of myself.

Mick had the spotlight swiveling back and forth from side to side of the river which glowed like pooled mercury. That's how we caught the yellow eyes of deer lapping at the water, frozen, surprised at how quick we rounded the corner and came upon them. There were little water varmints swimming along the banks too—muskrats, weasels, and river otters. Often, we saw the outline of full-grown, farm-fed hogs lumbering through the untended brush. At the speeds we were going we saw a flash of them, the arch of a dark shadow where the heft of their bodies stood out against the night.

The current leaned up against and parted on large rocks which I steered wide of without slowing down. When the boat's port side dipped into the river on a turn, the lantern revealed the submerged rock, but it was too late. The contact pitched me from the steel umbilical of the throttle and I flew ahead of the bow and damn near got run over by the boat. Mick got launched twenty feet through the air and crashed into the thick mud on the lip of the river. I was floating in an eddy with my life jacket propping my head up when he stood to look for me.

"You okay?"

"I'm not sure."

He had a mouth full of what looked like algae-slicked mud that he fished out with a hooked finger.

"It tastes like there's a party in my mouth and everyone there is throwing up," he said.

Floating on my back, a feeling of being so truly alive—ancient, familiar—welled up inside of me. I shut my eyes and prayed for the feeling to buoy some essential, sinking part of my life.

Fall:

The money ran out before the last round of bills for Nedra's rehab came due and if we didn't pay the bills we couldn't get the prescriptions for the medication she needed. Mick already gave me a loan for the second round of payments, and there was no asking again as work had been slow for him too.

"We could cut the Christmas tree forest. Loggers will pay good money to have at it. We have some of the best hardwood in the world in this region." I said to Merriam, but she gave me that disgusted, you're-less-than-a-man look that boiled a wild urge in me to start swinging that axe handle myself or, wilder still, drag her back to the truck by the river.

"Find something else," she said, ending our conversation there.

Then Mick got a big dry-wall job sub-contracting at a soon-to-be-shuttered coal power plant in Dunkirk. He could pay me for a few days of work so I drove out there and we split a room at the Motel 6. At night we ate in the local diner where most of the plant's single workers ate. The town was trying to reinvent itself and they had signs up that said, "We'll get to the future on the back of Nuclear," and a couple for and a few against a proposed site to store the waste from all the nuclear facilities in the country. Neither of us knew much about what was going on there, but I imagined that soon there would be spent rods, glowing green, cooled in underwater ponds; instead of hundreds of little radioactive dumps scattered around the country, there would be one spectacular tragedy against the environment, consolidated, in our backyard.

One night I called Merriam from the motel.

"How's Nedra?"

"She's not changing." There was an awkward silence between us. "How's it going out there?"

"Fine."

"You making any money?"

"Not a lot."

"Can you work more?"

"Can we please sell off the trees? Let someone cut them?" I asked again, but her silence screamed her disappointment and I hated her all over again for it.

In the surrounding towns there were little signs staked in the yards condemning nuclear energy, warning that some of that contaminated cooling water could get into the watershed and taint the Allegheny Aquifer. Most I saw were riddled with buckshot holes.

I drove back to Olean a day earlier than expected and contemplated the world we were creating—one in which my meth-head daughter would soon be soothing her scars with radioactive water that seeped into the river. She'd drift in the current beneath the shadow of the giant wind farms and wait for a glimpse of the feral pigs her father filled the woods with. I prayed she'd find forgiveness for my inadequacies as she floated towards the true shape of her life.

It was dark when my headlights lit up the base of Merriam's hill. The taillights of her Dodge pulled out and started down the back side of the ridge heading toward town. I followed her, thought maybe we could meet in town and eat together at the twenty-four-hour Egg and I Diner. But then she pulled off the road to town and veered west to the county line. I turned too and drove behind her in the same sort of trance long drives always put me in. When the homes started getting more and more frequent she took several turns into a neighborhood development and parked in front of one of the houses. I pulled alongside the curb a few houses down and from a block away saw the halo of her overhead light jump up as she opened the door and her long left leg swung out of the cab. As she slammed the door shut her hair fell loose across her whole back. A lean man with a long stride, orangutan arms, and parted black hair walked out of some front door and wrapped himself around her, placing his chin on her head before leaning down to kiss her.

A quick fantasy about slamming the accelerator, hopping the

curb, and running them down overcame me as they turned shoulder to shoulder and glided into the house.

The night deepened around the truck in front of that stranger's yard. My mind was wandering and I suppose it needed to land somewhere. Days went by without a single thought of the river, but at that moment the scent and color of it swooped down on me like a dark heron. In the truck the river pulled to me. It was moving through the county, measuring the wide swath of darkness and I wanted to be on it—beneath the eyes of resting birds in the trees and the open sky. Along the banks was the silent wall of trees yellow with swatches of fall, full of vermillion and burning ocher. Everything but the shores and the dark waters drifted away until Merriam came outside alone several hours later. She bounced across the yard, jumped up into her Dodge, and did a U-turn so she was heading back towards me. As she got closer I switched my cab light on. The shadow of her head angled toward me and her brake lights tapped red for a long moment and then off as she sped up and drove away.

After staying there for several hours, unsure of what to do, the sun came up. In the full light of morning I drove to Olean to find Bill Harrison, and lied to him about having the right to sign away the lumber on Merriam's land and filled out the papers like they were another divorce document. After the papers were signed, I drove on the back roads, past the Coptic Church and the shoddy grandstand where they raced old school busses until I was almost out of gas. Then I went back to the trailer and lay down in bed where I slept in short fits. Each time I nodded off I dreamed I was a snake being carried over the treetops in twin talons beneath the bony wing of a giant black bird.

With no work, all my time was spent prowling the grounds around the trailer and the house. Watching Merriam kiss that stranger had made me heartsick, useless, and weak, and that drained most of the anger out of me. We didn't talk about it, as saying anything would have meant sharing the feeling of utter hopelessness, which I couldn't do, as I wanted to be strong to help Nedra, whose body and mind were doing horrible things to her and kept her sleeping day and night. I couldn't bear saddling her with any more troubles. She was in her slug period. She slept fifteen hours a day. When she was awake she had no appetite, and dragged herself to the front porch where she sat with that thousand-yard stare fixed on the giant Christmas trees. I wanted her to go to community college, then to the local Franciscan college. I wanted to save her life, to drop it back into her lap like some glowing rod that would spark something inside of her.

Over that next week, Merriam and I let quick glances fall over each other and then looked away. When it was time to take Nedra back to Chautauqua for a checkup and therapy session, I didn't go along. The lumber company was scheduled to start cutting the forest later that morning. When she returned she'd see how deep she'd hurt me. But the part of me that hurt the most, the vindictive side that made the call to Bill, shrunk up when the men with trucks and machinery showed up.

They had two large excavators fitted with serrated pinchers for forestry work, and a giant Volvo feller buncher that cut and caught the trees in one motion, laying them down for the excavators to sheer branches and load into the trucks. Several dozen men, including Samuel Bergman, Sugar, showed up wearing embroidered jackets that said *Harrison Lumber, Making Every Tree Count,* and they worked fast, sheering off a layer of the forest from north to south, pushing back the line of trees before turning back and cutting more. Most of the day the forest roared with saws and trucks, which made me loathe my decision by the time Merriam and Nedra got back.

Their Dodge had to swing wide in the driveway to escape a departing truck laden with logs. Merriam got out and walked right up to me. "This is a crime against your family," she said, and she and Nedra scurried away into the house.

The noise of chainsaws on the property was everywhere. I shut my eyes and listened to the Christmas trees, bound for cutting sixty years ago, finally be eaten away. Harrison would make every tree count and so would I. The money from the trees could send Nedra to the community college for an associate's degree. She could do well there—she could get aid to go on. It was at least a chance and a chance was worth their combined scorn.

Later in the day I walked to the back of the house and saw them sitting next to each other looking out the window. They were sharing a thick comforter. Nedra had her head on Merriam's shoulder and it was clear why Mick would want to sneak up to the glass and watch these women. When I turned back to the collapsing woods I half expected to see him running away, chased off from the shelter of his natural longings.

Several days after the trees were felled I took Nedra to the river to talk to her about going to college at the start of the next term. It was secluded beneath the colorful parachutes of fall cottonwood and willow trees and that made me feel guilty again for the lost Christmas trees.

"Your mother thought you might want to talk to me," I lied, wanting Merriam's stamp of approval to make my daughter open up to me, but she didn't say a word.

"You know I love you," I said, needing her to believe those words.

The sound of the water calmed me enough to try again for some connection.

"It's okay with me whatever you are."

"And what am I, Dad? I thought I was your daughter."

"I mean. You were with that woman." Her eyes were burrowing into mine. "And the drugs. But whatever all this is about, you're my daughter and I'll do anything for you."

"Now you're here for me, huh? Isn't that convenient," she said. She began walking away from me, then stopped next to the thick trunk of a cottonwood tree. I could see her shoulders rising and falling with each breath. Then she turned back. "I always wondered what would happen if you lost your truck, if you'd be around more or if you'd still be an emotionally-removed, absentee father."

She'd never used those words before. They had come from her rehab, some therapist, but the words shaped her feelings and found their mark on me. Then she turned again and worked her way through the trees back towards the house. I wanted to call out to her but I didn't know what to do or how to fix anything.

After a prolonged quiet I kicked off my shoes, peeled off my pants and shirt and waded out to the icy depths of the river. The cold water against my skin was the closest thing to the electric joy of life that Nedra must have felt filling her body with amphetamines. Out past the sand ants and the Jesus Bugs flittering on the surface I let the current sweep my feet out from under me and carry me downstream. I latched onto a rock with my hands and dangled like a perch facing upstream and let my body levitate in the current, my pale white feet fluttering behind me. Nedra, I understood then, had gotten hung up on similar rocks and some fierce barbs in that awkward place between childhood and what came after. She stalled out and couldn't cross over. Under the water there was only a steady, thrumming whoosh. There was no room for anything other than wanting the next wild gasp of air waiting above the surface. Near the rocks the sound churned and whorled with a constant roar that swallowed any screams a man might be letting out beneath the Allegheny.

Winter:

In late October, I got a job as a tow truck driver and began tooling around town waiting for a breakdown or fender bender. In town the slow swirling gray chimney smoke crested the rooftops, curled through the branches, and drifted off in high columns on the wind. In the little borrow-pit ponds, the silhouettes of geese floated on the surface, their necks bent back and tucked tight on their bodies. At night I drank flood liquor in my trailer. Though when the first big storms hit on Interstate 90 and cars couldn't stay on the road, I started running the truck without sleeping, stopping only to get warm. Between Erie and Buffalo, hundreds of cars slipped out of the rut of exposed road and the snow pack pulled them into the median or spun them off to the side where there was no getting out.

In December, we got an Arctic blast that plunged down from Canada and frosted the western part of the state at night. It got so cold in the trailer one night Merriam even let me come inside the house for the evening.

Mick came over too and we built a fire. Mick and Merriam were drinking, but I had to work the Interstate later that night so I didn't. I didn't trust myself to drink around them anyway. After unhinging my jaw and swallowing so much disappointment, I was sure if I drank, all that would slip out and I'd say or do something terrible. But as the night crept on, Mick and Merriam got deeper into a bottle of vanilla-flavored vodka and I could see Merriam's mood begin to darken.

"Got to keep warm," Mick said, tossing a shot back.

"It's so cold because this one cut all the trees and there's nothing to block the wind," Merriam said. There was that familiar sharp barb to her voice that knifed under my skin and touched a raw nerve at my core.

Hadn't I driven trucks for years for them? Hadn't I been trying for months to find work for them?

"I wanted to see who was out there in the woods," I said.

Mick's eyes hardened on me.

"You're an incompetent, is more like it," Merriam said.

Her words sucked the air out of the room and I hated her for following through on her desires with someone else. I hated Mick for whatever desires he'd chased that led him to my daughter's window. I hated my daughter for inhaling chemical smoke that ate away at her brain, even if it was my fault in some way, even if I was a terrible father that crushed some weight-bearing part of her.

"And you're a slut," I said to Merriam.

"You have no right to call me anything. I don't owe you anything at all. We don't have to care about each other's feelings anymore. That's what a divorce does. It frees us from each other."

"You guys sure look free of each other," Nedra said.

"Nedra. Sit there and shut up," I said.

"Hey, Levi, watch what you're saying," Mick said.

"What does any of this have to do with you?"

"I'm just saying, you're being rough."

"That's my business then. This is my family, you pervert. You're lucky I haven't shot you in the backyard yet."

"What the hell are you talking about?" Merriam asked.

"Why don't you ask him," I said, pointing to Mick, who put his shot glass down and stood up like he wanted to walk to the door.

"What the hell is wrong with you, Levi?" Merriam said, and

something twitched deep inside of me. After months of trying to hold everyone together, I'd sucked down too much of the hurt that had slammed down on me. It was time to shed the life we'd had. My wife and I were finally done. My daughter's life was perched on a fine blade between recovery and regression. Mick was a lost soul. I was locked in a struggle to fend off a deep depression that would flatten me if I didn't do something. Mick must have seen all of that flaming across my face.

"Calm down, buddy," he said.

"Don't buddy me. How can you buddy me when you've been with my daughter?"

"What?" Merriam managed to breathe out.

Mick put up his hands and his eyes darted to Nedra.

"What is he talking about, Mick?" she said and turned to Nedra. "What happened? *Tell me!*"

Nedra's face turned sheet white and no more words were needed for Merriam to see what her silence meant.

"Oh my God," Merriam gasped. "Get out of my house," she yelled, and I didn't know who she was talking to. "You touched my baby, you bastard. And you, you knew about this?" She wound up and threw her glass at Mick who ducked as it shattered against the stone hearth. Then she stepped forward and kicked me so hard in the shin I fell backwards and toppled over the wooden rocking chair.

"You bitch."

"Mom. Stop it. He didn't molest me or anything."

"What the hell happened, Mick?"

"She came on to me," he whispered, his secret truth floating across the room.

"I felt sorry for you," Nedra snapped.

Then Mick's eyes narrowed and those knots of muscle at his jaw line tensed. "I hate you, you dyke," he yelled, like everything in him needed to explode.

"Don't you say that," Merriam said.

"You're a sad old asshole," Nedra spit back.

"You touched my daughter. You've been coming to my home after doing that?" She turned to me. "You let him come to my home after that?" She was trying to line up where to put all her rage. "What the hell is wrong with you, Nedra?"

"Maybe I've got daddy issues," she said, a nasty smirk spreading across her face.

"Do you not care who you hurt?" I asked, and then saw my words scrape through her ribs.

If nothing else I had sparked off a purging of our deepest wounds. I'd given them a voice which was something they had never had before. Then Merriam was walking around the room yelling, "*Shut up. Shut up. All of you shut up.*"

The burning logs snapped in the fireplace and for a stupefying moment Merriam stood rigid. Then her body seemed to lose its stiffness, her anger turned liquid and those unseen maladies drained from her into the floor.

They all began to grow distant then, as if everyone in the room was being pulled away.

Mick walked to the box of liquor bottles near the door, pulled out one in each hand and walked out of the house. His lean frame filled the succession of window panes on the side of the house as he trudged toward the clear-cut field without bothering to hide his familiarity with his path through the vanished woods. The three of us in the house remained there in silence. Nedra let herself fall backwards onto the couch. She wrapped the thick blanket over her shoulders. Her face was flushed a deep, deep red. It was a good sign, like at least she was feeling something again. I felt the sudden urge to run my hands over her arms, start at her shoulders and rub down to her wrists, over the little pocks and skin discolorations where the scabs had been.

We sat in silence until Merriam cried herself to sleep on the easy chair and Nedra nodded off into a restless sleep soon after. Then I stoked the fire and got dressed in a gray zip-up sweatshirt and green Carhartt jacket. I stuffed a knit cap down over my ears, put on my big neon green reflective highway jacket, and went back outside, knowing someone had to make some money for our broken family.

The Southern Tier Highway led me west to Interstate 90 along the train tracks, the river, and toward Lake Erie. It was so cold the train company sent out people to ignite the switches on the tracks to keep them from freezing, and off in the blustery distance were parallel lines of fire, arching flames glowing above the dark fields. It was past midnight when I dropped out of the hills onto the plains and pulled into the state troopers' office to see which side of the road they wanted me to clear. One of the troopers told me to head west and pick up the first vehicle stuck in the snow and keep going from there.

The first car was a sedan with a thick layer of snow on the roof about ten yards off the road. It had that little pink strip of tape blowing around on the antenna that said the police had already been there. I pulled alongside it but noticed yellow flasher lights winking on and off ahead of me and drove to take a look. The fresh tracks getting snowed over led to a Subaru Outback that had slid off the shoulder. From the angle of the tracks it was lucky not to have flipped. There were footprints in the snow where whoever was inside pushed their way out and paced back and forth until going back to the car. A man wearing a big fuzzy hat with a wool snowball dangling off the top rolled down the car window and started waving his arms and yelling.

"I have a kid in here," he said.

I helped him and his young son, who looked to have been crying, and was bundled in a Nike puff jacket, climb up to my truck where they squeezed in and watched me hook a chain to their front axle. The electric wench pulled their car out of the snow enough to use the boom to mount the car onto the wheel lift. The icy beams of headlights from other cars were still whishing past too fast for the weather which was good because I was getting paid per vehicle towed.

The father kept shaking his knee up and down. "I wasn't going that fast," he said to me. "I wasn't." His voice sounded disappointed in something. Himself I guess, his inability to get his son through the storm.

"It happens," I said. He looked at me like I was some hill-jack, and he was probably right. I didn't blame him for thinking of me as stuck in secluded irrelevance, rank and file with the other nothings out here in the middle of the country. He led some other life and none of this was part of it. They were on their way to or from somewhere so much different than this.

"I wasn't going that fast. It's just, look at this, look at it," he said, sort of disgusted with the snow blowing sideways over the fields. Something in his tone made me think that he was one of those men who think this part of the world is flat, in the same way for a long time I felt my life was flat, but that isn't the case. The rails blaze through the night, the fields bubble and dip, there are subtle bluffs where the soft gold-and-purple light of the evening lies down on the frozen corn fields, tracing the contours of everything until it reaches the river that cuts through the heart of this whole place and swells over the steep banks. I wished I could tell him this was as much a part of his life as what he had planned for and saw coming with polished promises from such a great distance, but he wasn't ready to hear that from me, and I wasn't sure I could have found the words yet anyway.

"Just look at this," he said again, holding his manic gaze as I carried him and his son safely away.

HOW WE DISAPPEAR

Paula wants to yell and let her frustration hiss and crackle out over the line. She's been calling like this since the house went on the market. Every time there's a visit that doesn't end in an offer or at least a follow-up, these calls come. The house is the last financial link between us, and she wants the money to turn full force into her life without me.

My dog, the fifth dog I've had named Taft, comes and lies at my feet as Paula lectures me about how to clean the house. Taft is a hundred-and-fifty-pound Newfoundland mix with black and white fur and a head the size of a go-cart engine.

"You have to go somewhere else when there are walkthroughs."

"No problem." I start to run the dog comb over Taft's fur. His undercoat comes out in finger-length clumps.

"I want the sale," I say. "I'm not obstructing any visits."

"Good," she says from somewhere outside of Santa Fe, where I'm sure she dreams of dissolving this last connection, our home by a creek that flows into the Allegheny River—sold off to the highest bidder and split 70/30 in her favor as per her blood-sucking lawyer.

"Rea will be over later today," she says, "so clean up and clear out."

"Sure thing."

I've filled half a plastic grocery bag with dog fur by the time I hang up. I walk the whole house pulling fur from the bag like smelly cotton candy and distributing it on the floor where it will be visible enough that anyone would be turned off. Taft follows me and gives me his sad, take-me-for-a-walk eyes. I haven't walked him in days.

The realtor's name is Rea Davis. She shows up two hours after my ex-wife's call. Rea is a plump, triple-chinned lady who's wearing a pleated brown blouse and gray pencil skirt that makes her look upholstered in carpet. She has thick, meaty calves, and smells of rose water and vanilla. For nothing she's done, but her mere presence in my life, I hate Rea. Her eyes make me irrationally angry, like she's some Gaul come to pillage my home.

Rea arrives with a young couple and their agent. Rea's face drops a little when she sees me sitting in the back by the creek with Taft. My feet are resting on a white dinghy my son, Charlie, used to float downstream in. The dinghy is chipped and dented at the bottom. Charlie used to climb in, wave good-bye, and call hours later from a payphone to tell me where he was so I could come and get him. Over and over he'd round the oxbow of the stream and disappear.

Taft wants to go greet the couple, but I hold his collar. His tail thumps the ground. They wave at me. The man has a thin black beard, and the woman is Filipino, raven-haired, and pregnant, show-ing but not uncomfortable yet by the looks of her easy stride into my home. I think, check out all that dog fur, all those allergens.

They are inside for twenty minutes. Too long. I imagine them looking at the pictures on the wall. Charlie growing from room to room. Me getting older. A few of Paula when she was young and before her head filled with sand. Then they come outside. They admire the trees, the garden, and walk to the retaining wall at the edge of the property; it drops eight feet down into the river.

Taft is whimpering to go say hello to the strangers. Rea gives me a polite little wave. The bearded young man wanders over to me. I recognize this thing he is doing: he wants some insider information.

"You have a beautiful house," he says.

"Thank you." I know this; it's my house.

"Where does the creek go?"

"This flows into the Allegheny River. It keeps going down to Pittsburgh."

He scans the banks.

"Interesting setting," he says.

Across the stream are two large properties hidden in summer by the full canopy of trees. Beyond those houses is an Egyptian Coptic Church with a gold dome, and a no-frills redbrick Lutheran church with a parking lot where a dozen bagpipers gather on Tuesday evenings to practice. Beyond the church is an old wooden wall built to blot out the sound of the Southern Tier Highway, which can still be heard as a muffled thrum cut by the high-winning buzz of crotch-rockets.

"Does the water get much higher than this?" The young man points to the little boat at my feet. The water is a slow babble over the stones now, six inches deep beneath the retaining wall and several feet where it fans out at the curve in the bank beyond my property. In the spring it floods and hops the wall. My backyard has had a current moving through it several times, and I've had to keep Taft on a leash to let him out. Of course I tell him this.

"Turns into a class five river." I let this sink in. "In fact I'm worried it might be crumbling away the concrete wall there." I point to the wall holding back the yard. He looks at his wife and the real-estate agents. I think this ought to do it for him, and I'm happy when he walks back to his wife and they all start back to the house.

So far I've pointed visitors to the crack in the rusted AC unit by the bedroom window, the proximity to the highway, and the flight pattern of thunderous planes coming and going from Buffalo/Niagara airport. My goal is to make it through the realty season without an offer. Not to keep some link between myself and Paula, but because I fear this place is the last tangible link I have to my son.

Paula calls that night. She holds nothing back.

"The dog is shedding. What do you want from me?" is what I say.

She hangs up. I understand why she does it. I'm being difficult.

I look at a wall of pictures. Charlie's a sweet, pumpkin-headed baby and a lean, pimply boy in hockey gear, before becoming a thick-necked, somber young man who was always in trouble. Then a soldier. A marine. Muscled. Stern. Unaware of how soon his dark fate would call on him.

Taft is scratching at his ear, and I give him a tap with my foot to get him to stop.

I go into Charlie's old room. The only thing in there is an old Buffalo Sabres poster, a bed, and my hockey equipment. I coached all of Charlie's teams despite knowing nothing about the game when he started. Now I play in a fifty-five-and-over league. There's only four teams, which I think constitutes all of the men in three counties who've made it this long and can still skate. The games are on Tuesday and Friday nights and checking and slap shots aren't allowed. It got to a point where hockey was all Charlie and I had to talk about. That's probably why hockey is one of the only things in my life I still love to do. The equipment stinks to high-hell, which is why I've been keeping it in Charlie's old room in sight of visitors and not in the garage.

It's mid-July, after a series of rainstorms, when it gets so hot at night, it's hard to sleep. I sit outside and tend to the fire pit to keep the bugs away. I'm sore from skating. My calves knot up. Ankles throb. The hum of 18-wheelers on the highway never stops. Every few minutes a plane rumbles overhead. Their lights cut a white cone from the dark sky. Maybe it's because my time sitting next to the river is coming to an end that I really pay attention to the place.

In the summer, animals from Allegany State Park pock the muddy banks as they follow the stream beneath the overpass, wind under the ramp and climb the banks to wander the neighborhood. Deer, opossum, skunk, weasels, songbirds, raccoons, and recently wild hogs that drive Taft nuts at night. He senses or smells them out there. Though it is in the winter, when the stream freezes, and food in the woods is sparse, that the coyotes use the ice path as their highway in and out of the edge of my property where Taft goes ballistic, giving them a primal growling fit that starts deep in his chest and reverberates through his whole body. He is inconsolable at these times and can't be dragged from the window when they are out there. Sometimes they come in twos and hunker close to each other under the evergreen. They wait and watch the house, listening to Taft and trying to sense what danger him and I watching mean to them.

When the fire starts to burn low with the last of my cord of wood, I wade into the stream and sneak through my neighbor's yard. I cut through the parking lot between the Coptic and Lutheran churches and cross Frontage Road to the section of wooden wall in disrepair. Some of the higher boards have fallen. I pick up two eight-foot wooden planks and carry them under my arm back to the fire, and

I listen to see if the highway is any louder. For my next fire, tomorrow night, I'll bring a crowbar and pry loose new boards. I'll do this until I can hear every movement from the highway, every avenue of change. I know I should have done this earlier. With Charlie. Shown him how his life could have led so many other ways. A sin on my part. The sin. I gave up on him too early. Wrote him off as troubled when he was just young, energetic, and unfocused. I suggested the Marines. Paula was against it. Every part of Paula was against it. At the root of Paula's heart she cannot forgive me that.

At nine in the morning the phone rings. A call right at the start of business hours seems ominous, and I'm correct. The machine takes the call. It's Paula's lawyer.

"Hello. It's Ethan Cleary. We need to talk about your availability to show the house and the state in which it's being shown. Rea Davis has another round of visitors today and it seems like it would be best if you caged the dog and weren't on the property. I'll call again later."

"Guess I better clear out today," I say to Taft. I'm afraid of Ethan Cleary. He has made life miserable and the less dealing with him the better. He arranged it so that so much of the profit and assets from our family gas station and deli go to Paula that I will no longer be able to afford running it.

I mow the lawn. Then fry up a whole package of bacon, letting the fat sizzle and the grease fill the air. I feed the strips to Taft once they're cool. When the pan is full of grease I let it boil and evaporate so the house will smell for hours.

I pack up to go to Allegany State Park and spend the day fishing. The woods are huge and consist of one giant interconnected body of forest-lined water. I set up along a concrete fishing wall—folding chair, small cooler, white five-gallon bucket, and three poles in the water at once.

Mid-morning, a man walks toward me. I can see it all over the guy before he's even fifty yards. Kmart shoes, worn jeans, a red flannel shirt poking out under a five-dollar gas station sweatshirt with the symbol for Route 66 screened on the front. He's balding with sad gray puffs of hair fighting it out for which direction to point in. Two little poodles run behind him. One black. One white. The white dog already found a puddle, and its chest and legs are brown and wet. The man walks to the edge of the pond, nods, then strolls over, asks if I'm having luck, what I'm hoping for. I want to tell him I have very little hope left, though say nothing of the sort. He lingers. We talk. About bait—muskie need expensive lures and are a hard fish to catch. Yes. They are in these waters. Night crawlers for bass. Why I'm using leeches—for bluegill.

There's a pause. A fish story swap. A pause. That stench of loneliness is between us. The little black dog sits at the edge of the water by his side. The white one is rutting through the swamped marsh grass.

This park is full of lonely men. Most probably weathered a long history of unforeseen diversions and have playlists of disastrous relationships. I used to look at men like this one as a warning, a precautionary tale of how not to end up. Though now that my son vanished in a gruesome blast in some sandbox on the other side of the world, my ex-wife rightly hates me for pushing him into the service, and I have no one to tell these things to, I count myself amongst his ilk.

When I'm done fishing, I pack up and drive to my gas station. I have low wage workers run the deli and gas cash resisters for me but like to stop in once a day at the end of the Whetstone shift. At some point during the week it seems like most of the town stops into the store to say hello. Most I imagine have a hard time sharing anything of themselves. A bit of chit chat and company fills some need to connect.

When I arrive Levi is finishing filling up his tow truck.

"How's Nedra?" I ask.

"She's saving up her and my money to move away," he says and points to his gray hairs, which is a joke between us about what children do to their fathers.

When the old astronaut comes in for coffee I yell out, "How's space today?"

"Always expanding," he says. This is all we'll share though I want to pepper him with questions.

Over the length of the late afternoon, Brooks, the CEO of Whetstone, comes in and buys chips and comic books for his son. Sugar and his dad come to show off their rehabbed 1970 Chevrolet Chevelle SS they'd painted gunmetal blue.

"I'll see you at our game?" I ask Sugar's dad who watches all the hockey games from the bleachers.

"Yep," he says.

A kid named David Liang comes in and does a pretty poor job pocketing a candy bar, but I pretend not to notice. I had decided to do this until he is sixteen, then, if I still have the store, I'll hire him to work for me and try to get him to sign up for the hockey team.

I like how I've gotten to know so many people in my town from owning this store, and hate that I may end up losing it. I hate it for me and I hate it for everyone I perceive may take a small amount of comfort from the place.

Once I had three Franciscan friars walk into the store. They wore brown robes with white knotted ropes hanging off their waists. They were from Assisi, Italy, and visiting the college for a conference. They told me our college was world famous among their order.

After that I began taking Taft the fourth for walks along the river through the campus. It was such a beautiful place and the mornings there always began in mist. From time to time I'd catch sight of a friar emerging from the fogged-in quad and always felt like I'd stepped into some other era full of druids. It was fascinating to have such a place in our community and I started studying up on them. The first Franciscans in this valley came in the 1800s and only spoke Italian. They were trained to recite the sermon in English and sent out to spread Catholicism into the foothills with just that one speech from our language. They walked and rode into the hamlets using old stage coach trails. I imagine their long Sundays getting pounded by snow and heat as they came over those bad roads. I can't get the fact those first missionaries only spoke Italian out of my head. I get stuck imagining how they also had to perform the sacrament of penance for English speakers, and even those recent Irish who only spoke Gaelic. I do not know how well that would have gone. Though my bones ache with knowing how heavy it is asking for a very specific forgiveness from someone who cannot understand you.

When the college was built and used as their home base, the friars went out into rural communities and tacked up handbills about their sermons and hearing confession. I shudder to think of the confessions those friars would have heard from settlers and their hard lives. That those stories that festered with guilt until they were purged were how those friars learned their new language, which they had to filter and use to marry, and baptize, and praise the same people and valley. It must have been a hard life, and they must have felt their bones iron cast with faith to support themselves through it.

When I recently asked about the three knots on the friar's ropes, and found out about each of them represented their vows of humility, chastity, and poverty, I was overcome with the sad sense that I have come to those three tenants as well, but by time alone, and not by any active decision on my part.

When things settle down at the store I do a quick check of the pumps in front and the dumpster in back. In the winter I used to put a bunch of shovels and buckets out behind the gas station. When the plow packed up a giant snow mountain neighborhood kids came and dug tunnels. They used the water spout to fill buckets and poured water into the holes so it iced over and froze solid. They worked for hours, day after day, until they had a network of tunnels like little moles. They'd climb up the hill, jump into the hole, go sliding on their bellies through, and I never knew where they'd come out. This started when my son was a kid and I had our second Taft. It's a good name and I've stuck with it. Once my son got too old to play in the tunnels it had already become a thing that caught on and I always liked hearing the kids out there having fun. Taft the third had to be locked up as he'd go out and drag those kids off the snow by their snow suits. Children used to laugh their heads off as he dragged them across the parking lot. They thought it was funny. I knew his breed of dog is meant to save people in the waters off of Newfoundland, but short of an ocean, that Taft's instincts kicked in when children dug into the snow. Of course that was a while ago. Now enough mothers got on my case that Terry the State Trooper had to come ask me to stop the tunneling before someone got buried back there.

I drive home. In my driveway is Rea with the young couple I'd told about the crumbling wall. The woman seems larger. Her belly now arches a tight drum. With them is a large Mexican man wearing a tool belt and holding a meter-long level. He's telling them something about the house. I park on the side of the road up the street and watch what I'm certain is a conversation that will affect the rest of my life.

I think of ways to make the house look like a mess. Hook iodine to the tap water. Put food coloring in the toilet basins. If I can make it to the fall; people don't buy houses in the fall.

That night, when it's dark, and bagpipers have stopped marching, I put on my hockey gloves and wade across the river with a crowbar and flashlight. I make sure there are no cars coming and use my light to hunt along the highway wall for loose nails. When I find one low to the ground I start prying it away. Nails groan. I keep at it, pulling until I've got four boards down and there's a gap in the wall large enough for me to squat down and walk through. The gloves keep splinters from driving under my skin as I carry the boards back to my fire pit.

Next to the new bonfire I catch the scent of bacon coming from Taft's fur.

I don't ever want to leave this place. Though it feels empty since Paula took all the artisanal decorations, Amish quilts, and anything else colorful or soft, inside the doorframes are marked with the pencil etchings of my son's growth charts. The walls are scuffed with his energies and games. I dipped into the crawl space to check the sump pump and found BB gun targets taped up where Charlie and his friend engaged in an insane sort of gunplay that involved violent tiny metals ricocheting off concrete. This place marked time during his passage through the world and I long for it like it's already been yanked away from me.

On Friday afternoon Ethan Cleary calls. An offer was submitted to Rea Davis.

"We're going to go ahead and take the offer," Ethan says, as if it's his life on the scales. "Paula has given her consent so we'll need a few signatures from you, and we'll go ahead and deal with their financing."

I make myself an early dinner. I have one of my old-men hockey games tonight. I eat a salad with ground meat on top. I drink plenty of water. When I'm finished eating I sit at my table looking out at the yard. My fork taps the plate. A small defeated action.

At the ice rink, I go through the warmup and feel slow and groggy. Though there is something about breathing the cold air, the *huwhiet-huwhiet* of ice scraping away beneath my skates, and the chaotic rattling of the boards I love. The first period goes by frantically. I'm all over the place. There's no order or grace to my movements. The banners of the league sponsors flash past. Harrison Lumber. The Tavern. Whetstone.

With under seven minutes left in the second period, Gerry Donagen scores for our team to tie the game. When I take the next face off I feel a manic excitement working itself up in me. Loose and alive, I let everything beyond the ice go. I skate after the puck when a wingman intercepts a wrist pass at our blue line and has a break-away with only me to beat.

I skate right at him. A surge of anger rises, one that has been spiraling loose to only now show itself. I am going to bowl him over despite the rules. But the winger stops, sets his skates, and lowers his shoulder to brace himself—all in one fluid movement. His braced shoulder pad lifts me off the ice and knocks all the air out of me. The back of my helmet crashes down hard, and I spin across the ice in a long three-sixty on my back before stopping in front of the goalie crease.

From the ice the rafters look like the ribs of a giant whale that has swallowed me. I can't breathe, and there's that familiar cold against the back of my neck. The goalie looks down on me, but his face is hidden beneath a crimson mask. A blackness. The glove of my right hand was knocked off, and my pointer finger rubs back and forth against the ice. I can hear voices calling my name, but no words rise from me in response. I'm empty, unavailable, far away. It occurs to me this is another of the ways we disappear.

Our only fan, Henry, yells, "Breathe. Just breathe," from the stands.

My teammates help me off the ice, and I spend the rest of the game with my fingertips prodding at the swelling knot on the back of my skull. I'll be sore tonight when I'm home alone looking out the window with Taft.

The other almost-sixties skate back and forth in a patternless swirl. I shut my eyes, as even their slow pace makes me dizzy. The *huwhiet-huwhiet* of skates fill the air, and I see myself skating down the Allegheny River alongside the coyotes. I open my eyes, and my vision is still unfocused. I feel undone. When I shut my eyes again I am getting in my son's little dinghy and floating down the river. Taft is running along the banks as I flow into a new life. Though even half-concussed, I know it will look much different. More like a small U-Haul with the last of my belongings, pulling out onto the highway in search of that lurking shape-shifter, the phantom of hope.

THE DELIGHTS OF SOUTHERN FRANCE

Cline was in the storage room rooting out bananas again. When I took his mammoth hand in mine and led him away, his thumb rubbed over the bones and valleys of my knuckles. It was an innocent muscle memory recalling walking with someone he once loved. Because of that heartbreaking action, I was almost happy to be there to quell his confusion for a moment.

"I was shot in the war," he said. "Lost so much blood the doctor told me to eat a lot of bananas."

He must have been six-foot-five before his spine hunched, but he still looked capable of tossing me through the wall. I closed my eyes, took a deep breath, and didn't ask what war he was in.

In the kitchen, Rosemary saw me leading him and made to stand. Her back was hurting so I waved her off. I'd seen her lead Cline back to Ward C dozens of times.

"I got him."

"Thanks," she said. The stainless steel counter in front of her was so clean, her warped reflection slumped on the surface. Plump body, hunched shoulders, and a sponge of gray roller-curled hair captured under a hairnet.

The electronic door code in Ward C was 7195*, but they kept changing it because Cline was an escape artist. Nothing they tried kept him in. As I unlocked and pushed the heavy door back, the scent of bleached floors and soiled then laundered bedding stung my eyes. Cline shoved a fourth banana into his mouth. A clump of four more hung from his gnarled pointer finger.

Residents wandered the square unit's hallways. Tim the evening watch nurse's aide rested his head on the desk.

Rosemary would scream at Tim for letting Cline slip out but I could see Tim was stoned by his carny grin and squinty eyes. He had long frizzy brown hair and a thick beard braided into a rope and threaded through green, yellow, and red beads that dangled from his chin. He looked like a weary Jesus after performing at some Christian kid's birthday party.

"See you later, Cline."

A small woman stood in the way of the door. Her apple green hospital gown was backwards like a deep plunging evening dress that revealed the sides of her breasts. Her chlorine water eyes didn't blink. Her mouth moved but made no noise. She stepped closer and hugged me. I hugged back. When I let go, she didn't. Her eyes held that confused desperation.

"Okay now. It's okay."

I reached over her and punched at the key pad. I messed up the code and started over. Two more bent old ladies pushed their walkers toward me. I messed up the code again.

"Buzz me out, Tim."

"The doctor told me," Cline started while stuffing another

banana into his mouth.

The two ladies came closer and each reached out to touch me. A dry hand on my shoulder. A second clutched my elbow. A fear they'd pull something from me made me panic.

"Buzz me out!"

The three ladies were all barefoot. Their toes looked like chewed gum.

"Tim!"

When one of the last synapses fired in pot-addled Tim's mind and the door buzzed, I shimmied away from all three sets of hands and slipped into the hallway leading back to Ward B. I leaned against the beige paisley wallpaper and pushed down the overwhelming desire to change everything about my life. Cline's enormous head filled the Ward C door's window. His mouth was full, and he chewed like some gentle bovine.

In the kitchen there was always a To Do List. Rosemary made job charts for the succession of high functioning teens and low functioning twenty-somethings that worked there for as long as they could handle it before fritzing out mid-shift and leaving in tears. I was in the latter category, a twenty-five-year-old kitchen aide.

Rosemary wrote the dining room's seating chart in pencil. New names were scratched in over the ghosts of names that had been moved from Ward B, been hospitalized, or passed away and taken by the daily rounds of the ambulance to Olean General. When I first started working there, the seating chart made me so damn sad. I was sad to begin with. Everything in my life that had been promising did a fantastic about face and left me so battered and stunned that I went numb.

Ward C was for those who were still mobile but whose senility and Alzheimer's-rattled minds let them wander off and get lost or hurt. Those people drifted up and down the hallways day and night like insomniac ghosts.

In Ward B the residents had their wits still but their bodies betrayed them, and they couldn't move without assistance. Those people were wheeled into the dining room with the row of westward facing windows. It was snowing hard and wind blew across the glass. Snowdrifts climbed the side of the cars in the parking lot. The familiar sight of my father with his Russian fur hat and overcoat made his way past the cars to the dining room doors.

I gave a tray of food to an RN at table four so she could spoon-feed the five people at her table.

My mother was at table eleven. Her body, contorted by ALS, sprawled in a limp letter "S" on a medical bed on wheels. Her hair was blond going to gray, and she had the thinnest wrists. She chirped but was otherwise non-verbal. Her left hand leaned against her left thigh. The pointer finger on that hand was the only part of her body that still moved. It tapped her left thigh so much it irritated the skin there and scabs flaked off. Some days the leg was bandaged or bleeding and an arc of red was embedded under that fingernail. At her table, as I held her thin wrist and guided it away from her side, she tracked me with her eyes and chirped. She'd been there as long as I had but I still found no meaning in those noises.

Rosemary carried a dirty blender and walked into the dish room where the steam swallowed her whole.

When I brought another tray out, my father took off his hat and sat next to my mother. He trudged through snow, rain, and summer heat to join her for dinner every night. I placed bowls of food down on their table. He nodded and began serving her and the senile old lady next to him named Nelly who yelled and screamed through her whole meal.

"Now, now, Nelly," he said as he fed everyone. My mother's finger tapped her side. I liked to think she tapped in Morse Code. Some message. Tap, tap, tap. Get-me-out.

The wind howled against the windows. Nelly shook her spoon and flung sloppy joes across the floor. I stepped on the glop of meat and ground it into the microfiber carpet where it soured. Once the rest of the food was on their table, I got away fast.

My father was studying how to mercy kill my mother. It was his secret. I knew and decided to do nothing about it.

I helped with the dishes. The spray gun got hot enough to blister and often sheaths of skin peeled loose from my hands.

Dish runoff soaked the front of my pants. I felt disgusting and wanted to turn the hose on myself, let it get hot enough to peel everything away, hot enough to molt and emerge as something new.

The last task was to gather up the food pony cart full of dirty trays from Ward C. When the Ward C door opened, the half-naked lady who grabbed me earlier wasn't there. Several residents walked the hallways. One old man stood motionless and stared up at dust particles hovering beneath the neon hallway light. I walked the halls looking for the pony. People called out to me from their rooms. Mr. Paulson yelled, "Hi there, Twerp."

The pony was at the end of the east hallway and it was empty. Tim was nowhere to be found. He was never where you wanted him to be.

I went room to room gathering trays. There were two beds to a room and each had a desk next to it where people kept their personal items. Mail heaped up there was only checked if family members visited, which rarely happened. I thumbed through bills, letters grade school kids were forced to write to their ailing grandparents, and then the social security checks. I thought through different ways to cash them for myself. Several could have worked. But I pushed all that aside and went for the junk mail. Every resident had travel brochures sent to them. Exotic safaris, fall foliage trips, snorkeling the Great Barrier Reef. The brochures came from universities, AAA, and travel companies. Each offered a shock of color. I took those and held them flat under the dirty food trays so no one saw.

I left the pony in the kitchen for the morning dishwasher.

"Good night," Rosemary said.

I took my stack of brochures, grabbed a roll of tape, and clocked out. I walked toward Room 43 in Ward B.

She was still in her bed on wheels. I pulled her thin wrist away from her side and placed a pillow there so it wouldn't close back in on the same spot and make it bleed. Her half of the room was covered in glossy travel pictures. Dancers in Papua New Guinea with bones in their noses. Masai-Mara ladies with royal purple capes. A woman in a peach hijab adrift in a breeze behind her as she strolled across a mosque's stone courtyard. I was tired from my shift and daydreamed of being the man floating in the snorkeling photo on the wall. One giant breath then a deep dive. Down along the shafts of light to all those fish and reefs.

"I'll be right back," I told her and went to the laundry room with the giant dryers and had the night laundry man, Dennis, a sixty-year-old ex-convict with cauliflower ears, give me a fresh change of bed linens hot from the dryer. Back in room 43, I pulled the curtain so not to see her comatose roommate, Cora. I stripped down the old sheets, spread the fitted sheet over the mattress's plastic coating, and tucked in the bed sheet. I peeled it back so it was ready and pushed her chair closer.

"Here we go." She was so light I scooped her up with ease and paused to give her a gentle squeeze in case that's something she could still feel. I hoped the warm sheets felt good against her skin. When she was propped on the pillows I looked into her eyes. Soft hazel with chips of gold. I untangled her delicate gold chain where it lay twisted around her neck.

Chirp. Chirp.

Tap. Tap. Tap.

I leaned my ear to her lips. Breath wasn't good enough. I wanted her voice. An "I love you." Or just, "Love," a word I could chew on forever. But there was nothing.

"Got some new pictures for you." I pushed her wheelchair aside, sat at the desk in her room, and cut out the travel brochure pictures.

"This one's for a cruise on the Mediterranean. *The Delights of Southern France.*" I cut away the picture of handsome silver-haired retirees at a fine meal on the aft of a gigantic ship, but kept the picture of a field of lilac in lemony sunlight. I cut out all the snorkelers and imagined free diving again until the shrill dirge of Nelly echoed from down the hallway.

When I had a stack of cut out pictures, I taped them on the wall over the older pictures.

"A change of scenery."

I was still wet from the dishes but didn't have anywhere to be so took a book out from the stack under her bed.

I read until she was asleep. Her finger tapped at the pillow.

I put the book away, leaned over, and kissed her forehead.

"Goodnight."

When I got home, the Russian fur hat hung from its hook. I touched it. I'm not sure why. It was such a ridiculous-looking thing.

The bathroom door was shut and my dad was in the bathtub again. This was a new thing for him. I had never known him to take a bath or even relax, but over the last weeks he spent hours in there, draining the water when it got cold then refilling it.

"Hi Dad."

"Hi."

That was all.

In the kitchen stacks of bills lined the wooden table. The stacks were how my father and I communicated. What we could pay. What we had to kick down the line. Debt we had taken on. Where there was hope to take on more. Bills for our second mortgage which either got paid or we had to address the bankruptcy paperwork we'd tried to avoid. The snowdrift of my mother's medical bills was so big that both of us appeared to be crumpling under its weight.

The dining room floor was covered with my father's tools. He was teaching himself how to do electrical work to avoid paying anyone to do it. He'd changed all the light switches and power outlets in the house. The wiring in the dining room was pulled out and the load and ground wires reattached. He kept redoing that one until snippets of thin copper wire lay scattered over the floor.

In my room I stripped off my dirty work clothes and crammed my hairnet into an empty plastic pretzel jug full of hairnets. I lay down in my bed naked and looked out the window where the wind blew so hard I couldn't even see my neighbor's house.

Four years before I was in college at a local Franciscan university. I played on the club ice hockey team, had friends, and even a girlfriend, Anna.

After our hockey games I drank myself into an obnoxious oblivion it took me three days to recover from. It was very late one of those nights after the bars had closed and after hours drinking at the hockey house ended that I stumbled back through the campus by myself. The sun wasn't up yet but would be soon. Dense fog climbed over the surrounding foothills and cascaded over the sports fields and campus. Everything looked exotic and strange. I felt like the only person alive. Then one of the campus's dozen Franciscan Friars in a brown habit with a hood cut through the fog ahead of me. I didn't know where he was coming from or going so early but began to follow him. He moved fast and I was stumbling. I'm not sure why I felt the need to track him like that. My mind is always summoning me to make lonely ceremonies of random moments which feel heightened and worth dwelling in. He hurried between buildings, and then entered a forest trail along the river from one part of the campus to another. He went deeper into the fog and disappeared the way Rosemary did in the dish room steam.

It was the morning after following the friar I got the call from my father. My mother had been getting sick more than they let on. Neurologists confirmed the diagnosis a few months earlier, but they didn't want to tell me. They were telling me then because she had to stop working, and money had been tight. Tuition payments were becoming too much with the onslaught of medical bills, and we'd maxed out our loans. I listened to all this but still half drunk, and inching close to an epic hangover, my mind was still tracking the friar from the night before. As my parents talked through the reasons I would have to leave school after the semester ended, a year and a half shy of my degree, I began making my own triage plans. How to keep seeing Anna. Create my own reading lists. Stay in shape to rejoin the hockey team. Of course none of those plans worked out, and now I think that friar was absconding with my youth and potential before the dawn broke.

In the morning I showered, warmed up the pot of coffee my father left for me, diced up a banana to put in my Cheerios, and ate while studying our bookshelves. The three bookshelves in the living room were lined with research on ALS, handling insurance claims, insurance company flow charts, social security disability information, medical research, magazine articles on cutting-edge medical trials, manuals on nursing homes, the legal rights of the sick and infirm, law textbooks, western and eastern medicinal cures, homeopathic remedies, meditation guides, and music therapy books. After long enough, doctors consoling with potential breakthroughs no longer helped. What was left was hoping that in the tunnel of silence, her mind soared like a falcon.

In his closet my father hid books about Dr. Kevorkian. Legal assisted suicide. Oregon's 1994 Death with Dignity Act that was meant for people with less than six months to live. He'd studied actuary sciences, training manuals for morticians, and county coroners. There were case files photocopied from the library of different ways people have been killed or died and the reports surrounding those deaths.

He did not know I read those books too.

Before the impossible vacuum she became, everything pulled inwards, my mother asked us to not let things get "Too far. Too bad." She didn't have to tell us what that meant. She must have pleaded with him in their private lives as well.

"Eddie. This might fall to you," she said and reached out to hold my hand which I could not lift to give her. A mortal fear pierced the inner tissues of my chest. I stood there and could do nothing but tremble. I didn't respond. Cowardice on my part.

I'm not sure what she said to my father. My father is a quiet man. He's smart and well-read. He strikes me as someone who has plumbed his own depths and made his own sanctum of that space. His inner life may be fathomless.

I ate my cereal with bananas and scanned his secret shelf once more. In the case studies, my father had highlighted sections about the damning clues that shifted suicide investigations into the undetermined cause of death or homicide piles. That train of thought he let himself slide down was his way of feeling out some floor to stop our slow descent.

Among his hidden reading material there was also an illustrated copy of the Kama Sutra, with little stars and dates etched next to most of the pictures. A lifetime's worth of my parent's sexual explorations with each other felt like the most personal part of my father's secret world, but also the one full of vibrancy and life so, for that reason, I thumbed through it more than once.

Serving my mother gave life meaning. Sometimes I thought I'd take the registered nurse's assistant course to make a few extra dollars, play adult league hockey games on the weekends, bank my inner fires, and live there forever. But I also resented it. Other people didn't have to live with a moment by moment sense of loss. Loss of my mother. Loss of my time. The clock in the hallway becoming its own sort of torture. Tick, tick, tick. Loss, loss, loss. Tap, tap, tap. Second by second fading, hurtling past the dredges of my own youth. I was angry at her for getting sick. I wanted my parents to be okay. To live my own life. To experience what I knew others were doing with their time. Living. Loving. Reaching for what they wanted.

At the nursing home an ambulance was at the front entrance. The driver was a woman named Rachel who was friendly because I gave her loaves of banana bread when she pulled up to the kitchen's storage room windows.

"Any business today?" I asked, a gallows humor joke.

"Fredrick Lovell. Heart attack." She pointed to the entrance where her partner was filling out paperwork to make Mr. Lovell's final transfer.

"Is Mr. Lovell in the back now?"

"Yep," Rachel said.

I placed my hand flat against the side of the ambulance. A tiny ceremony.

In my mother's room she was still in bed from the night before.

"Good morning, Mom."

I pulled up the chair tight to her bed and started right into reading travel books from the Olean Library. I tried to find stories from the places pictured on her wall.

The wall of pictures made the world vibrant and alive. Maybe it was an extra touch of torture to show her places we'd never know. Those places waited for other people. I wanted to distill the entire planet into something small and tangible, to drop it into her one moving hand as a gift worthy enough to show her how much I loved her.

I started my twelve-hour shift. In and out of Ward C and the dining room.

My father walked in his Russian fur hat toward me and then later away from me through the snow. Cline in his daytime clothes walked past the dining room windows outside which made me laugh at the sad silliness of it. The RNs saw him and raised the alarm that he'd escaped again and all went rushing out of the room after him.

Back home, on the kitchen table all our bills and insurance forms made me want to set a match to them and let the story those bills told curl to ash. I imagined myself hoisting a burning table leg from the smoldering heap and carrying it outside through the cold. A lone light in the night. I'd walk to the glass windows of the nursing home and hurl it through one to let the whole place scorch. My dark imaginings were some unchecked need gone to rot, but I didn't care. Those daydreams burnt because they were all I had some days. I let the image of the meat-stained microfiber rug ignite and spread. There was fire and finality for many of those people and it was another burden on my shoulders that I begrudgingly accepted.

Though from that dark daydream came Cline, leading many of the residents out to safety. I let them go their own way and for once stopped wasting my own life in servitude.

I knew I wouldn't get a shower anytime soon so went to my room to change clothes.

I had the next day off but it rained, so I went through our bills organizing our next few months of payments, then watched movies on the couch until I fell asleep. The home phone rang late at night and woke me. I expected to hear my dad shuffling through the house. The phone kept ringing and then stopped. I got up to use the bathroom and the phone rang again.

"Hello. This is the emergency contact number for Mr. Rawls. He's been admitted to Olean General Hospital."

It was pouring rain. My back tires hydroplaned through a stop light but there were no other cars, so I pumped the brakes to get traction back and blew through the intersection.

I parked in the ER lot and ran inside. The receptionist told me where to find my father on the third floor. Each hallway reeked of mop water. He was alone inside a room and asleep on the bed. An IV bag was in his right arm and a giant bandage was taped over his forehead.

A nurse came into the room, walked to my father's arm, and placed her hand on his wrist to check his pulse.

"What happened?"

"He's been sedated."

"Why?"

"He was brought in unconscious. When he woke he started screaming about his wife and wouldn't stop."

"What happened to his wife?"

"She died."

"What?"

The nurse jumped back and stared at me.

"Where is she?"

"You'll have to ask the doctors." The nurse walked out of the room but I ran after her.

"What happened?"

"I'm not sure."

The hallway was too bright. Too many noises. Machines. People coughing. A pounding in my own body. My skin tingled and shoulder muscles went ridged. The nurse was saying something. The doctor would talk to me later when she's free. She doesn't know any details about my mother.

"She's in bed looking at the Masai-Mara," I told the nurse.

"Sir?"

I reached out to steady myself against the wall and moved by feel back to my father's doorway.

"Dad." He didn't move. I walked to his side and took his hand in mine. "Dad." I rubbed my thumb over his knuckles. His gold wedding ring was scratched but held my own warped reflection in it which I stared at until something else felt manageable.

When nothing came, I ran from the room and down the hallway, down the stairs, and outside into the rain to sprint through the parking lot to the car.

It was still pouring rain but the ambulance was in the nursing home parking lot. Rachel jumped out of her seat when I knocked on the window.

She cracked open the window. "What are you doing here now?"

"What happened to Mrs. Rawls tonight?"

"Oh, she's the same as yesterday, just no longer alive." She gave me her practiced gallows smile. "What are you doing here now?"

"Is she back there?" I nodded to the ambulance's cabin.

"No."

"Tell me. What happened? Please."

"Her husband came and gave her a bath. He had to use the bathroom while doing it but slipped and cracked his head on the floor. He was out when we found him. Tim in there called in a tizzy and when we got here the guy was in a puddle of blood from his head. His wife was on her side underwater."

"Drowned?"

"For over an hour or so. The alarm in there didn't work and Tim didn't hear anything. When he remembered to check on them, he freaked."

"Where's Mrs. Rawls?"

"I took the old man to the hospital. The coroner van came for her. Hey. Got any banana bread?"

I turned away and walked back inside the building. My feet sopped against the welcome mats as I ran down the hallways to Room 43. The divider sheet was spread out hiding both beds. I yanked my mother's aside. The bed was empty. Glossy pictures covered the wall. I scanned the pictures as if she could now be in one of them. Next to the bed on the desk was the gold chain she always wore. I brought it to my nose to smell it. Several cut up brochure pictures not yet taped to the wall covered the desk. I grabbed a picture of a snorkeler. I pulled back the second curtain and Cora was on her back with her eyes closed. Her breath was shallow and my bursting into her night hadn't startled her at all. I crammed the picture and necklace into my pocket and ran back into the hallway.

At the other end by the nurse's station, Tim stood behind the desk. His eyes were red and bloodshot but opened like his hyper vigilance now would make up for his epic dullness earlier.

"It's not time for breakfast," Tim shouted down the hallway.

I walked up close to him. "What happened?"

"I'm never covering a shift for Maxine again, man. Worst mistake ever." He pointed to the end of the hallway where a yellow police tape covered the bathing room door. "Total horror show."

I snatched his rope of beard and yanked it. He whimpered as I turned and threw a fistful of colored beads down the hallway. They bounced and rolled toward Mr. Moseys room.

"Time for breakfast?" Mr. Moseys yelled.

"Yes," I yelled back.

I went down the hallway.

"Don't go in there," Tim cried after me.

I tried not to look too long at the tub, or even the toilet, but went to the emergency button and leaned close to it. The wall was wallpapered and the emergency button held on by a plastic shield with a screw on each side, no different from a light switch. There was no paint or plaster that would have chipped off or drifted away if it was taken off and put back. I imagined how it unfolded. First as an accident. A long series of misfortunes cresting in this room on two people I loved.

I left the bathroom and roamed through the halls of forgotten people, pushed aside by their lives, families, or economic miscalculations. In the next ward, a nurse sung while brushing a wheelchair-bound resident's hair. Another nurse took a moment to dance with an old man who had managed to dress in a faded corduroy suit.

In the kitchen I took the empty pony food cart, pushed it into the storage room, and lifted a whole cardboard carton of Dole Bananas inside. No one paid attention to me despite my soaking wet clothes. I wheeled it into the hallway, down to Ward C, which had a new security code, so I needed to be buzzed in. The door unlatched. I wheeled into Cline's room. He wasn't there, so I pulled out the bananas, opened the box, and dumped the clumps on his bed. I wanted to impose something special about Cline's past. An escape artist from a vaudeville show. But I knew from his mail he worked for the railroad flipping switches for coal trains coming out of Dunkirk and Olean. He was no Houdini, just an old veteran with dementia. His mail was on the bedside table, and thumbing through it out of habit, I pocketed a travel brochure for a river cruise. *The Crown Jewels of the Nile.*

It was three in the morning. The laundry room still smelled of hot dryer sheets. I stripped off my soaked clothes, pulled a crumpled snorkeling picture, my mother's necklace, my keys, and wallet out, and threw everything including my shoes and underwear into the dryer and toweled off. I stood naked in front of the giant machine and wanted to climb into it, let it tumble me against the metal sides until I was too dizzy to think or feel.

At five thirty in the morning I walked back into my father's hospital room. He was awake. He saw me, let out an exhausted wheeze, and tried to choke back tears.

"I'm so sorry."

Blood had seeped through his bandage like a blurred rose.

"Dad."

Tiny red rivers coursing the whites of his eyes drained into his irises.

"The alarm in the bathroom didn't work," he said.

I dug in my pocket and pulled out a crumpled picture and my mother's necklace. I handed the necklace to him, and he cupped it and brought it to his nose. I studied the crumpled cruise ship advertisement. Teal waters. The large black fins of a snorkeler. The little tube of air to breathe and breathe and breathe.

His face held no telling flicker. I considered the quiet purpose of his hidden books.

"Now what?" I asked, like maybe all I need was a vision for a livable future. I wanted to talk about my mother. To hold some spark of her being up between us.

He turned away from me.

"What did she do at the end?"

My father put his hand next to his leg and let his finger go, tap, tap, tap, and I don't run deep enough as a person to understand what messages could have been conveyed between a married couple in such a moment. The TV mounted in the corner of the room was off. Our drama played out on the dark mirror of the screen.

THE NAMES OF WIND

The men in my life are sea captains. My husband, Alex, writes me cryptic messages on postcards he sends from all over the world. The latest came from the Philippines. It says, "I want to have a better relationship with you." I wonder what he was thinking when he wrote it. On the front of the card is a picture of teal waters running up a white sand beach that looks like it has never been touched. Alex's father, George, had placed it on the kitchen table, probably wanting that note to be for him.

George is sitting on the couch watching the Sabres game. The crown of his head is bald and the white horseshoe of hair he has is so long he wears it in a ponytail that hangs to the middle of his back. His white beard is bushy and drops below his chest bone. My son, Ryan, is on the couch with him. They have riffled through the mail looking for acceptance letters from colleges Ryan applied to. Ryan wants to go to The Maine Maritime Academy in the fall. George made a call to friends of his there and told them to look out for Ryan's application. George told me this like I would be happy about sending my only child off so far. I want him to go to the local Franciscan college, to stay close. Though Ryan has been hounding me every afternoon, "Mail mom—any mail?"

"No school letters," I tell him.

"Any day now," he says, disappointed by the prolonged knowledge of his fate. And holding the postcard from the Philippines, I know the choice he'll make.

"Did you ever send strange notes like this to your wife, George?" I ask.

"Yeah. I did all sorts of strange things," George says, patting Ryan on the shoulder and laughing. "I called her once in '78 from Neuse Correctional Institution in Goldsboro, North Carolina to tell her I wouldn't be home for eight months."

"What did you do?" Ryan asks, looking over to his grandfather.

"Don't talk about that kind of stuff, George," I say, knowing how much Ryan looks up to him.

Alex had told me about his father being arrested when he was a child. How when Alex was growing up, his father consisted of stories he'd share after each stint at sea or in prison, and how those stories seemed to be where George lived his real life, not at his home. Alex was still angry with George for a whole array of things he had only hinted at. As a younger man George was a heavy drinker, and got off the ships so pent-up, he'd binge when he got home, knocking over whatever peace had settled in his absence since the last episode of purging his craziness. Alex's anger with him is still so palpable George only visits when his son is away.

George has a place on the east coast north of Portland, Maine, and when he retired he bought a small Winnebago he drives to Olean and parks in our backyard and lives out of during his visits. I have an extra room for him, but he says he doesn't want to be a burden, though I think he likes having his own space.

I go into the kitchen and hear George telling this story to my son: "The ship I was working on as a third mate at the time was boarded in The Port of Wilmington and the customs officials found the bricks of cocaine one of the crew members was smuggling from Hong Kong, so we all got arrested."

"George," I yell from the other room, and they stop talking, so I only hear the television. I pull on rubber gloves and began scrubbing the sink with a Brillo pad and think about Alex.

Alex is now the captain aboard the *M/V Coral Sea* out of Trinidad. It delivers cars from Japan to the rest of the world. George is sixty-eight years old and has run every sort of ship on the ocean to every port you could find on a map. Ryan wants to be like them. I see it in the way he follows his grandfather around every time he visits and the way he asks questions to his father over the phone to hear about where he is and what he's doing.

I want to copy Alex's postcard and give it to Ryan. I'll make hundreds of photocopies of it and send them to him when he goes away. I've always been able to handle Alex being gone because I had Ryan. And four years ago, when George first showed up with the raw look about him that said he had come from somewhere where he had put in some pretty hard time, he helped keep me company. He had apparently decided to reconcile his life with his son's family, even if his son wouldn't forgive him. But when Ryan leaves I don't expect George to visit as much. It makes me think of what used to drive me before having Ryan, and for all my efforts, I can only remember foolish goals which no longer interest me.

At night, I write on Alex's postcard, "I want you here," and put it in my drawer with all the others. I go to bed and read my book which is about the ancient library at Alexandria, so I don't think about my husband looking out at the beach on the postcard.

The phone rings late.

Alex knows when he calls to talk to me for a while, so I wake up enough to start talking as well. He's in Singapore. He tells me what has happened on the *Coral Sea*. What the crew has done in ports. I lay in bed and listen to his voice and picture the little crow's feet at the corners of his eyes from years of watching the sun's reflection off the water. He has spent the majority of our married life eradicating any romantic notions I may have held about a life at sea. He tells me now how he spent the day wading in the bilge waters which were contaminated by oil and engine leaks, brackish and thickened a rainbow slicked brown color. How his ship's crew is so small he's had to help unload trash and load provisions. They'd all gotten in a line and handed things to each other. When they unloaded the trash from the locker they tied bandannas around their faces to stunt the stench of garbage heaped in a hot metal locker for a month. The bags were heavy with foodstuff rotting inside them. There were maggots. He tells me the shifts he's working are leaving him exhausted.

"Do you miss me?" I ask, wanting to hear something about his feelings.

"I do," he says. "Didn't you get my postcards?"

"I got a few," I tell him, knowing this is the extent of what he will tell me. He was in ship mode and there are no soft edges to that life. Everything on the ship is rusted or shorn off, sharp and unforgiving. I hear it in his voice—he is wound too tight, and seeking comfort from me will not work at such a great distance. I have heard it enough now I believe something happens to him when he has been alone for so long, like he has forgotten how to let others back into his life.

I can't sleep after he calls. I look out the window. Sometimes the clouds here don't move and the sky is soft and frozen. But most nights the wind picks up and screams down from the foothills and makes our house creak. The noise keeps me from going back to sleep.

I sit under my yellow Amish quilt and watch television downstairs and flip through the channels. There are infomercials for jewelry, lawn care products, and exercise machines on. I let myself think the commercials are in real time, and these sales people are in front of a camera at this moment and not sleeping either. There is a rerun of the local ten o'clock news. The main story is a twenty-nine-year-old woman who died while inner tubing down the Allegheny River that runs through our town. This time of year the river is cold enough to knock the air out of a person. She was submerged for over two hours before the fire department found her body downstream. It seems a cruel trick of fate that a short visit to the river cost this girl her life, but back in 2008, Kate Spitz swam the entire three hundred and twenty-five miles of the river. I'd watched that story on the same news program. I turn off the television. Then there is only the dark corners of the room and the time until morning which always makes me want to run away to places like those deserted beaches.

I find myself thinking of sex. I've found myself in a long period of wanting. Often it's a wanting to have Alex back. That makes me think of how far away he is. I think of all the stories of dangerous situations he's been in over the years, and the ones George has told me about. The life they live is so far removed from anything I'm living. Everything they've been through makes me feel like there are accidents everywhere, and they could happen at any time, from any direction. Sometimes in streaks of paranoia I feel like they are surrounding me, fighting to see which one will land first. It makes me want these men who go so far away and come back with such wild stories safe and by my side.

I have been so lonely I found myself wandering a big box pet store looking at puppies. There were so many different kinds, I had no idea where they all came from. The place felt like a financial monument to our need to pour love out of us into something. Pets. Our work. People.

George wakes up early. He makes breakfast for us and acts like a father to Ryan, as though this late in his life he feels the need for family or tradition. I walk downstairs and hear him talking with Ryan.

"What are the women like?" Ryan asks.

"You should see the women," George says, then stops talking when he sees me.

Hearing him I feel this deep ache as real as any broken limb. I think of Alex, and how he had told me the Filipino crew mates of his knew where every whorehouse in the world was. It was something I always thought about while Alex was away. He'd come home with this eager sex drive like a madman which I loved. I can never imagine how he suppresses all that want when he's gone. I've imagined him laying on some sultry bed in a far off port, an exotic and younger woman walking towards him. She smells of lavender and sweat. She straddles him, but he rolls her over, so he is on top the way he likes. The thought makes me want to swim with the drowned girl from the news underneath the cold river.

George has eaten before we got up. I look at him and can't even begin to guess all the women he's been with. It makes me nervous thinking of Alex screwing me out of his memory on the other side of the world.

I want to tell Ryan he doesn't have to live like his father, or

George, who I now want as far away from my son as possible.

"Do you mind checking to see if the paper came, George?" I ask. George walks towards the front door. "You don't have to do what your father does," I tell Ryan.

"Mom——," Ryan holds his hand up to me, refusing what I want to say again.

I want to tell Ryan what he never hears. His father could mark where on the map he was when the major events of his family took place. He was sailing to Iceland from the Shetland Islands when one of his younger sisters from his mother's second marriage had her first child. His mother fell down the last step into the den and broke her leg when he was off the coast of Belém, and he remembered thinking that was the start of her going downhill, which it was. His other sister had twins when he was off the coast of South Africa; it was a difficult birth and one of the twins did not make it. His mother died when he was in the South China Sea, and I had Ryan when he was mid-way through a crossing of the Atlantic Ocean.

George brings in the paper. I toss aside inserts for the local dancing horses show, an ad for Harrison Lumber tree services, and reminders of the annual artisan fair and antique car show. I find myself thumbing through the pages to read about the drowned girl. I can see myself at her funeral. The casket will be closed because water does horrible things to a body.

After breakfast George and Ryan take their bikes for rides along the river. They will come back with little gifts for me. It's become a habit for them. They bring me wildflowers by the handful or chocolate bars they get at the corner gas station's deli. It's something George and Alex have always done when they pay off of ships. They bring me unusual decorative art or exotic foods, like they need to buy their way back into my graces. The flowers from Ryan feel like a training for when he leaves in the fall.

When they leave I wait for the mailman to come. When he does I go out and thumb through what he has brought. There are two manila envelopes. One is full of the photo shoot work I did for Whetstone's winter catalog. The other envelope is from the Maine Maritime Academy. It's thick like there's a stack of paper folded in half inside. I want to tear it up and scream. Rejections come in small thin business envelopes. I shove the rest of the mail back in the box and keep the photos to review and the maritime academy letter.

I put the envelopes in my book and grab a towel. I walk to the trail along The Allegheny River and find a place to lay out my towel beneath the trees. By the river path there is an older lady with her dog. The dog walks into the water so its four paws are under the surface and it laps at the water. I wonder if it can smell traces of the dead girl still shifting under the surface.

On this trail I once found a pigeon with a little scroll on its leg. When I got close enough to try to reach out and grab the note it flew off. Another time a giant golden retriever hurtled out of the woods, jumped up, and licked my face. I grabbed his collar, which said "Ralph" and a local phone number. When I took my belt off to use as a makeshift leash he bolted into the woods. Then when I saw a huge farm pig, which was all dirty and awful looking, I ran away from it because I couldn't stop thinking of it biting my face.

I reviewed the pictures I'd taken of the chrome-plated knives. I'd used my favorite Kodak, and they came out nicely. The CEO's wife was in the studio that day, and we got along well. I took a few pictures of her holding up the knives like a model. The pictures will take a little cleaning up on Photoshop and will be ready for their new catalog.

I read my book. The spine opens at an odd angle because the Maritime Academy letter wedged between the pages. The chapter I am on is about the last known librarian before the library at Alexandria burnt to the ground. Hypatia was her name. I think of her being the gate keeper to all knowledge and wonder of the ancient world and what she must have known by occupying her seat. Hypatia had to wonder what information would come to her next.

Reading about her brings a loneliness over me. I find myself guessing whether she had secrets of her own or did she only gather and hold the knowledge earned by others. Besides part-time work doing graphic design at Whetstone, my job has been to help keep my house clean and ready for my men to come home to me and tell me their stories. To them I am the ancient librarian, the collector of stories, and I sit at the throne of our family's knowledge of each other. Because compared to them I am sedentary, they cannot also see I am the drowned woman—the whore crossing the room.

I reach into the pages of my book. I take out the Maine Maritime envelope. At the edge of the river I pick up a stone the size of a grapefruit. I put the envelope on the water and put the stone on top of it. Under the water the envelope looks like fast food wrapper. I know what it will say and what that will lead to. The academy will make Ryan cut his hair as soon as he arrives. He'll come back to me with a crew cut, older and itching to go further and further away.

Later that night I set the dinner table. George and Ryan sit down and are talking.

"So when a cadet gets out of the Academy are they ready to captain their own ship?"

"God no," George says. "It takes a long time to get to that." His voice is authoritative and precise. "All the times I was scared on a ship sort of hardened me into automatically doing what was necessary to fix the problem. It became a habit and reflex. That's why you have to put so much time in that you stop being surprised when the moment of strangeness happens, because you are the one in charge of everyone else at that point."

"George, can we please not talk about my son being in danger?" I ask.

"So how long did it take you to get your fourth stripe?" Ryan asks.

"It took me years of waiting for ships in union halls and a lot of setbacks to make captain," George says. "I had to take a lot of crap jobs as a mate before that happened for me."

"Is that why things didn't work out with you and grandma?" Ryan asks.

"Ryan!" I say, surprised at his bluntness. We never talk about those things.

"I'm sorry," Ryan said. "Was that bad to ask?"

"No, not at all." George looks at him for a minute, then at me. "It's okay," he says. "What happened was it was never easy for me at home. I'd come home and sulk around the house in a poison mood, trying to get used to being around people I loved again."

This older man's voice hints at the stories Alex told of his father. Alex claimed George could turn and snap with such viciousness that Alex was always afraid of him.

"Well, what was your favorite place then?" Ryan asks.

George tells Ryan and I about the whiteness of the Arctic and Antarctic, the bright blue of the sky and of the light reflecting off the water in the tropics—the greens of the shorelines, and the brownness of the desert streets in Africa during his days in Ghana. It was clear the things he had seen somehow touched him deeply and led him away from any sense of home he may have had. The world he went out into was so immense that I think he has no idea how one small place can also be fathomless.

George keeps telling stories. I watch how Ryan listens to him.

"The Doctor almost took us down," George says.

"What's the doctor?" I ask.

"The Cape Doctor is the strong southeast wind that blows off the coast of South Africa. It was blowing so bad the waves took out our engines, and we were floundering. Our top cargo deck was full of lumber containers that were shook open and wood planks blew all over. A six by six board got blown up and shattered the pilot house windshield so the cold and the wind was getting in and soaking up the consoles."

"What did you do?" Ryan asked.

"I almost crapped my pants." He smiled at Ryan. Ryan used both his hands to push his straight blond hair away from his eyes. "That was the first time I felt a heightened sense of survival that I have since seen in a lot of otherwise indistinct people."

"What do you mean by that?" Ryan asked. I listen to him and think of the manila envelope under the water.

"Yeah," I interrupt, "but George never went to a regular college, so he can't tell you about how great those are."

"Mom," Ryan said, "he's telling a story. Let him finish."

"At times," George continues, "it's not uncommon for men under the duress of losing their lives to pull off some feat of ingenuity and courage that saves everyone. That time it was me dumping our starboard side fuel and potable water tanks and manually steering from the aft levy console, so we rode heavy side into the storm so the wind didn't push us over."

"That's not all either," George said. "We had to get towed into

Cape Town after that storm. While we were there we kept hearing on our radios ships off the coast were seeing all these floating planks of wood clumped together on the water, like we'd laid down a boardwalk."

The story George tells makes my bones ache for Ryan. They did when I was pregnant with him, like my body wanted him to be alive more than anything. The image of Ryan walking over wood on the water flashes into my head as we sit at the table. Below the wood is the drowned girl whose funeral I read will be Saturday, at the Lutheran Church.

The phone rings.

"I'll get it," Ryan says, "Dad said he'd call today to see if I'd heard from schools." I hear him talking on the phone but I can't make out the words. He comes back in the room carrying his high-tops. "I'm going to play basketball at the gym." He leaves and I sit at the table with George. We sit together. George will leave before Alex comes home. When they are together their past is like a third person in the room they cannot make peace with. It makes me sad for Alex who cannot forgive and for George who only wants to be forgiven. It makes me worry about how children look at their parents, like if the parent's need for their own lives will be held in contempt by their children.

"I'm sorry Ryan got so personal there, George."

George looks at me like he is trying to speak. "That's okay. For all that life with other people I missed, I'd get off those ships and didn't want people around me anymore, like the world was too tight. I couldn't explain it and I wish I could have changed it, but I couldn't."

I can now see it's the same with George as it is with Alex—how nothing passes through him, and everything that has ever bothered him balls up in his stomach, and how he wears all that stress in his shoulders. I didn't know what questions I could ask to understand him and Alex better. When Alex was home he'd treat me with great affection between long stints of disinterest.

"What was it about your time away that made you like that?" I ask him. We have never talked about his life beyond his adventurous stories before now. Ryan asking about his wife must have jarred something loose in him.

"Life on ships is compressed. The pace of change is constant which is addicting, but you get to a point where you feel like you've done everything. Seeing and doing everything eventually makes you tired of everything, no matter who you are. Then you're around all kinds of people who are the same way, hard, and you have to have something crazy happen to excite you, and that isn't healthy. I gave into the tiredness for a long time. Trying to reawaken yourself to life is a very hard thing to do. That's how it went for me."

"Why did you go away?"

"Well, I went into the Navy and became a pipe fitter which got me out the door. And when I was young I guess I wanted too much. It always felt like the things I wanted were staring as hard at me as I was at them my whole life, and they never met. It's probably the only thing I passed onto Alex."

I sit with George like we're a married couple, he's my older husband, or at least fills in for Alex in his stay. I look at George's arms. Alex and George are both covered in tattoos like totemic clan signs, so even in their silence their bodies tell their stories.

I sense all the sadness of having lost his family to his restlessness and feel a pain for him stabbing at my midsection. It's like we both know his years of stories have amounted to very little. Though I wonder what more do I have? My stories are of a home. To stay busy I had my photos and design projects over the years. I bought a whittling kit and shaved cedar blocks into crude little horses that left curled pittings all over the porch. I started basket weaving, and I planted gardens with flowers and then vegetables which I put into jars. I know petunias and blue asters. I know how to make over a hundred different dinners. I know how to make my husband come in four minutes if I want him to. I even got a paint by numbers kit and copied famous paintings which made me understand what it must have felt like to have created something great. Though looking back on it now it's like I never had much of a career. And now I will only have taking pictures of knives and this house for men to stop into to fill their need to be somewhere when they are not at sea. Though even when they are here, telling these stories, sometimes I know everything about them with one look. Others, they are strangers to me, and I ask who are these men, and I know the world is so swirling and large beyond my bubble. When Ryan leaves in the fall, I know I will feel a senseless vacancy, and the flatness of life without him ahead of me seems eerie.

When George gets up to go to his Winnebago, I tell him, "I'm terrified of Ryan going to sea."

"What?" George says. He turns towards me. I know he didn't hear what I said.

"Good night," I say.

In the morning I take my book back to the river. A yellow bi-plane whines by overhead. A fan boat speeds downstream. There is an ice-blue gleam off the water in the boat's wake. I wish the men in my life saw all the interesting parts of this place that I'm tuned into. I could tell the stories of this place to them. How Arthur Miller used to stop in Olean as a young hitchhiker. How Thomas Merton studied and wrote at the local Franciscan college, and drafted *The Seven Story Mountain* there, inspired by these hills.

I read about the last known days of Hypatia and the fire at Alexandria. I imagine the liberation Hypatia must have felt as she watched everything burn. I finish reading and walk north along the trail. Giant English elms line the upper riverbank and cover the water. Across the river is a dirt path mountain bikers use. I see George standing at the base of one of those giant trees. He's looking up. Over seventy feet high in the tree is Ryan.

Seeing Ryan in the tree heightens my sense of things. I stand on the bank of the river that cuts through the woods. The sun burns everything yellow and the yellow flame rests so soft and stunning on my son's blond hair that I have to squint. The sound of the water rushing over the banks below is coursing in my veins, and the smell of holding Ryan after I'd delivered him when he was still covered with my blood fills my head. This is what life smells like, I had thought then. Ryan jumps off the branch, far out over the middle of the river and for one moment he's flying. *My boy can fly. My boy smells of life and can fly.*

His long blond hair bunches around his head as he is held suspended at the terminus of his jump, and then it chases him downwards at a sharp angle where he falls forever, slicing feet first into the water and disappearing. I run to the side of the river and feel all the longing in my life focused on one point where he splashed under.

"Ryan!" I yell, and the sound fills the empty pocket where he had lived inside of me.

"He's over there," George yells from the nook of the tree Ryan has jumped from. I look up at him and he has his shirt off, his hair is unfastened, and his white beard covers his whole chest. He is pointing downstream. I look and see Ryan climbing out of the cold water by grabbing exposed roots in the muddy riverbank. His long arms and legs move so fast he is standing at the top before I can let go of my panic. He waves to me with an enormous smile as he walks back towards the tree he jumped from. I follow him with my eyes, and when he walks behind the tree I see George is halfway up it himself. He is wearing shorts and his bare feet look like they blanket every contour of the bark as he pushes himself up.

"George, get down from there!" I yell. "Ryan, get him down."

"We do this all the time, mom," "Ryan says.

I hear voices coming from upriver. A group of people on tubes float towards us. Their pale legs stick out of the black tubes which are shining in the sunlight.

"George!" I yell as he climbs higher. He's at least forty feet off the ground now, and fifty off the surface of the river. He turns himself around on a branch. His hand supports him on the tree, and standing straight up his bald head is a luminous piece of rounded glass and his beard is crystalline white. His body still looks strong but hangs down flabby at his biceps and stomach. His tattoos look like giant faded skin growths. He looks like one of those men in religious paintings from my paint by numbers kit. He looks like a trucker version of Moses or God. "Get down from there George!"

"Your mom's going to have a stroke," he smiles down to Ryan.

"Mom," Ryan yells across the river. He is resting in between the major trunks of the tree. "Watch how far out he can jump."

I hear the pride in Ryan's voice.

"What do you think Ryan, should I jump on these folks?" George says pointing to the tubers headed down stream.

"Do it," Ryan says.

"George. Don't—" I yell as he jumps from the branch. His beard covers his face as he falls. From where I'm standing I have no depth perception of how far out he'll come and I think he may clear the whole river and crash at my feet. He splashes under the surface and is swept downstream towards where Ryan climbed out.

"God," one of the tubers yells as George splashes in front of them. They must think God has fallen from his perch. I hear Ryan laugh at the tuber, and when I look up at him he is climbing back up the tree. I know he is following the route George must have laid out for him—that this is how it must work for men. They follow the paths their fathers and grandfathers leave.

I watch Ryan climb back towards where he jumped and know Alex had followed George despite all their craziness and inability to communicate, and Ryan will follow the mystery of his father's life. I shut my eyes as Ryan jumps again and see the deep enormity of the ocean the way Alex has told me about it—the islands of clouds stretching miles up into the atmosphere and the hideous shadows they cast, and the wind that shakes it all. I see George, Alex, and soon Ryan telling someone the names of all those winds. The names of currents and air streams they have all set ships in groove with or worked against, navigating the mouth of the horizon which opens and breathes out its many great blasts.

THE BROOKS RANGE

Brooks didn't know where the boat was when he woke up to the familiar sound of Adler sobbing. The boy's grief was a night-blooming flower, bringing him these crying spells several times a week for the last six months. During the day, Adler was eager for the highlights of their trip. But with his ear to the steel deck of the Alaska State Ferry, the wind snapping the sides of the tent, and the slow, steady thrum of the props four decks below, that unknowable pain, some mixture of confusion and powerful understanding, roiled loose in the boy's sleep.

Brooks reached out and rested his hand on Adler's shoulder and gave him a shake.

Adler shot up and stared at his father. The salt crust of sleep was in his eyes, and he smelled like a pile of leaves, damp earth, and nutmeg. His head bowed, as if making a wish.

"Why'd you wake me?" he asked, his dream already beading up and rolling away.

"What do you need?" Brooks asked.

"What?"

"Can I do something for you?"

"Let me go back to sleep."

Brooks studied Adler's face, looking for some trace of whatever gargoyles took hold that far down in such a young boy. Maybe it was a gift to let these things play out in depths he could not get to. But Brooks feared that what ate at the boy and was keeping him silent would poison some part of him if allowed to fester. He had hoped being away from constant reminders of what they'd lost would help deliver them to some plane—a plateau to stall the free-fall they'd been in. But in the dark, rocking their way as far north as either of them had ever been, he lay watching his boy and tried to fend off the lonely truth that his son already had a private life he would never know.

When Adler was asleep again, Brooks dug around in the backpack at his feet and pulled out a stack of papers sealed in a giant Ziploc baggy. He snapped on his headlamp and read what his wife, Teresa, had written.

Teresa had been pretty, skinny, with washed-out blue eyes, crooked teeth, and a small pit in her left cheek that somehow added to her feminine appeal. In his mind, she came to him as he saw her the summer before. He'd been washing the dishes and looked out the kitchen window over the sink and saw her and Adler talking on one of the Amish quilts that looked like it had a giant orange eye in the center of it. He wore a red and blue knit cap. She had on a green headscarf. By then, they'd been told she didn't have much time left. Teresa and Adler were pointing up at the clouds. To Brooks, their arms wavered like lone blades of prairie grass. It was a simple and clear moment he hoped Adler would remember and harbor good feelings over.

She died at the start of December. Ovarian cancer. It happened at Olean General. It was the middle of a sunny winter day. Red and yellow leaves still fell in the light outside her window. He put her fingers to his mouth and kissed each one. The soft electric hum of machinery filled the room. Power cords. IV drips. Computer fans. He shut his eyes and felt like he was sliding off the side of the world. When he had a nurse bring Adler into the room to say goodbye, the boy, twelve years old, pulled the bill of his Sabres hat down to his nose and began hyperventilating. Brooks kneeled in front of his son.

"Do you want to try to say anything? That you love her?"

Adler couldn't catch his breath, so Brooks hugged him and led him away. Life had yawed, chance and terror had touched upon the womb of his wife, and there was no knowing what his son needed at that moment, as they began gathering in this new absence.

They'd moved to Olean for him to take the CEO position at Whetstone. They rented the house because he had planned to uproot and move the company as soon as the clock on an old "No Move" provision ran out at the start of the new year. It was an easy decision. Three southern states had offered insane tax breaks, new factories, the promise of nonunion labor, and they could keep the "Made in the USA" label. Or he could shift production overseas and make enormous profit margins. He had both sets of proposals ready to show the board. Then his wife got sick.

At the funeral many of the Whetstone workers showed up. At first he was angry with them, thinking they were sucking up. That thought was buried under profound grief. Then, after the service was complete, many in the crowd walked up to Adler, and not because Brooks was the CEO and lost a wife, but because Adler was a boy who lost his mother. They offered him gifts.

A line worker named Jeremy handed over a starter socket wrench set. Bruce, the old founder of Whetstone, gave an envelope with a World Encyclopedia set by subscription in it that would start with "A" the following month. The company's photographer gave Adler a photo of Teresa holding up a knife in the factory's studio. On the back of the photo was note that said, *Your mother was beautiful.* The old man who owned the gas station and deli near the factory gave Adler a kid's hockey stick. He must have sat through the whole service holding it in the pew. A boy named David about Adler's age laid down an already opened tin of Skoal bandit tobacco dips, which Brooks pocketed and tossed in the trash on the way out the church door. A local pilot handed over a NASA pin and a replica of a yellow twin engine bi-plane.

After the funeral when he took inventory of all those gifts, and decided they were the strange shape the people's compassion took, he decided to shred the proposals to move the company. He would keep the factory where it was.

After that his colleagues from the Whetstone factory, family, and friends reached out, but their attempts to comfort him left Brooks exhausted. He decided to take a leave from work and left the daily operations to Brian, the Chief Engineer, so he could be with Adler. It was then that he printed out all of Teresa's old emails. He had kept an email file named "Teresa" and for years stored any notes from her that were cute or loving, or held some tremble of her personality. At times, he'd open them and track the day-to-day shape of their love among the busy business of work, childrearing, and keeping a home. After she died, he printed out that entire file of emails at a late night copy center. It took two reams of paper, and he kept them in a box under the passenger seat and in a small stack in a baggy in his backpack. Each night, he took out a day's worth of her emails and read them. He would pretend, close to sleep as he was, like they came from her that day.

After three days on the ferry working toward Yakutat, Alaska, a small fishing town full of bearded men dressed in disheveled, mismatched clothes and knee-high slicker boots, Brooks and Adler camped in a small campsite for summer travelers off the ferry dock. They prepared their gear for the wilderness rafting trip that was to be the centerpiece of their summer on the road. They took pictures of the shore and of each other, hair tussled by the wind, pointing off in the distance, scanning the horizon for the triangular cut of orcas skimming the surface.

"Look at this, Dad," Adler said, running from the woods behind the campsite. He held out the bones of a foot-long bird's wing, eagle or raven. "This looks like a baby pterodactyl wing."

Teresa would have told him to drop the bones. That touching them was unclean. Brooks could hear her voice, the excitement and revulsion over what a boy brings forth to show his mother.

They ate a dinner of hot dogs and canned white beans cooked over a campfire.

"This is the best meal we've had in a while," Adler said through a wad of chewed food.

"Hey. I cook some good meals at home."

"Well. Sure. But you know what I mean."

They watched the pastel and crimson colors leaching from the sky at sunset. Stars rose up and Brooks and Adler made wild designs over their heads with their fingers, giving their connect-the-dot constellations their own funny names, *The Incredibly Long Wiener Dog, Orion's Ugly Sister, The Warty Foot.* They read in their sleeping bags using camping headlamps. Adler read his video game and WWE wrestling magazines, both full of muscular, cartoonish figures. His bookmark was a flyer of a dancing horse show from back home that had a picture of *Maiden Priscilla* in a skintight sequin body suit. Brooks was sure Adler ogled the picture on the flyer.

Brooks read Teresa's emails. And late that night, when his son woke them both up with his weeping, they stared at each other in the strange midnight light filtering through the tent flap.

"Adler. Buddy. Please tell me what's going on," Brooks said. But the boy put his head back down and either could not or would not speak before falling back to sleep.

When Brooks and Adler arrived at the pier on departure morning, they got their first glimpse of their guide, Andrew, who was a squat, rugged man, with a salt-and-pepper ponytail braided down to the center of his wide, powerful shoulders. He was at the top of the pier, hugging a dark-haired woman and a little girl with the same complexion, and waved goodbye and blew them kisses as they got into a rusted two-door pickup and drove away. The little girl was yelling, "Bye-bye Daddy." Andrew turned back and walked toward the group.

"Brooks and Adler, I presume," Andrew said.

"That's us," Adler said.

"You guys picked the best time of year for this trip." His silver tooth glinted when the sun found the back of his mouth. "Let me introduce you to the crew. This here is Kurt, a first-timer like you guys, and that is June, who's done this trip with me three other times."

Kurt had a thick mustache, and wore a crew cut, military-grade lace-up boots with camouflage cargo pants, and a button-down denim shirt. His brown eyes, dark, unblinking, and looped by shadows, were focused on neutral space as he shook hands.

Next to him was June, who was a foot taller and twice as wide at the shoulders as Kurt. She had fishbowl glasses that magnified her eyes, and wore a pair of enormous hiking pants that zipped off into shorts. She swept up her internal frame backpack with two fingers and flung what Brooks guessed to be a sixty-pound bag over her shoulder with ease. She stuck out her dimple-knuckled hand to Brooks and Adler.

"Glad to meet you, fellas," she said with a slightly Southern accent.

Adler smiled, looked down at his shoes, and his face reddened. There was something about the woman's stretched putty face that made her look angry.

That morning, Andrew checked and repacked everyone's gear and moved it all to a float dock, where he had already loaded his own gear into a floatplane.

"Any connection to your name and the fact we're going into the Brooks Range?" Andrew asked.

"Not that I know of," Brooks lied, not wanting to share anything of himself or his past.

His father had served a stint in the Coast Guard, stationed in the Aleutian Islands. On a furlough home, he ended up flying over the tundra and saw the opening to the Brooks Range, which he said was the most spectacular place he'd ever seen. The name or the image stuck with him and he gave it to his son.

They took an eight-seat, twin-engine, King Air floatplane from the dock. After nearly two hours in the air, they landed on a lake in northern Alaska, in the heart of the Brooks Range; the plane would pick them up after ten days of floating a section of the Kokolik River.

In the plane, looking down on the mountains, the cloud cover broke and the wilderness revealed itself. Emerald-green valleys half in shadow. Fierce slabs of exposed granite. Crystal-blue glaciers and white rivulets of waterfalls streaming down the slopes.

The doubt that he could navigate his son through such a place—through life—came again.

Adler was glued to the plane's window, and Brooks tried to shake loose the fear such wilderness brought him and remember that this is what he'd wanted—a chance to give Adler the wonder, the essential miracle of the world. This was so different from where he came from. In Olean, he had ached for wild places, for such stark geographical features to make him feel peaceful and humble, as opposed running the factory which made him feel frantic and small.

Andrew pointed out the left side of the window to a river that cut a serpentine path through the wild topography. "That's where we're headed."

Adler looked at his father and mouthed, "Holy shit." Brooks had hoped bringing the boy to open, wild places would help him purge whatever ill feelings were knotted inside of him, and if this was the sound of that happening, he was okay with it.

The plane dipped even with the mountaintops, descended along a river valley, and touched down in a wide blue lake. The pilot taxied twenty yards from land before cutting the engines. He got out and walked onto the pontoon, pulled an anchor out of a forward hatch, and dropped it into the water. Andrew climbed after him, and they opened a cargo door in the back of the plane and pulled out a deflated raft that was tied together, using heavy cords and pulley locks. Andrew began inflating the raft from an oxygen compressor stored in the back of the plane. Brooks and Adler watched as Andrew slid the oars into the oar locks, placed paddles and all of their gear into the raft, and pulled it alongside.

"We're ready for our adventure," Andrew said, as he helped each of them take a seat on the rubber sides and then pushed away from the plane. The plane's motor started up. It began careening across the lake, lifted off, and drifted up and out of sight before they stopped hearing the trailing whine of its engines.

That familiar wave of uneasiness descended out of the endless blue sky and onto Brooks.

"You guys relax for a bit, and I'll get us to a good spot on shore to make camp for the night." Andrew was standing at the back of the raft. He rowed across the narrow lake. The mouth of the river was a glowing flood of mercury, silver in the light, black in the shadow, translucent when looked directly upon, revealing the perfectly-rounded stones lining the bottom. Rainbow trout with brightly-colored flanks flittered in the babbling current.

Andrew pulled the raft to the bank. "We'll do a small portage here to avoid a nasty set of rapids and then make camp on the other side of the spit of land." He looked over at June. "Do you want to do this one again, or do you want us all to help you?"

"I've been dreaming on it since last time," June said. She grabbed the ropes along the side of the raft and lifted part of it, using her arms and prying the rest of it with her knee. She dragged over five hundred pounds of gear and raft, while emitting graceful, feminine grunts, as she muscled it all over the portage. Her golden arms heaved the raft over the sandbar, and each footfall left a print two inches into the ground.

"That's my girl," Andrew said. He winked at the guys. "She loves to show her true strength out here."

The first camp was on a fan of white rocks along the riverbank. Andrew staked out a hundred-yard triangle. One point for their sealable toilet bucket. The other for their kitchen and to store food hung from bear bags in the trees. The third for tents placed in a semi-circle around a fire pit and his own tent. He slept with a large bore rifle to ward off bears and wanted to be closest to everyone in case of an issue.

"He wants us to be eaten first," Adler joked.

Brooks and Adler shared their two-person tent they'd been

using since leaving Olean six week earlier. It was sturdy and water-proof, with a yellow awning. Kurt and Andrew both had similar tents—Kurt's blue; Andrew's brown, with a green tarp. June's was a one-person bivy sack tent, with a top flap that zipped back to leave the mesh roof open, should she want to sleep under the stars.

Andrew stepped into the stream and walked until the water was hip-deep on his brown rubber waders. Hatches of tiny midges clustered in pockets of sunlight over the water. He walked upstream, casting the fly over his head in graceful figure eights, the fly whistling past his ear before he tossed it into the eddies, where a felled pine sieved the stream. Brooks and Adler hiked up a switchback trail and peered down at their raft, the thin finger of smoke from their camp-fire, and the colorful bulbs of their tents.

"Take that," Adler grunted and pitched a stone as far out as he could.

"And that," Brooks said, putting his whole arm into starting a game with his son. He rotated his arm to loosen his shoulder. "Arm's not what it used to be. I'm falling apart."

"Don't say things like that," Adler said, his voice sharp enough to break the easy tenor of play.

An hour later, Andrew had a stringer full of luminous river trout he'd cut open and let the river clean free of entrails. He hung them from a low-hanging bough and ran his fingers along the dangling fins like they were a wind chime. Then he wrapped potatoes in tin foil and pitched them in the bedded coals and fried the fish for everyone in a long-handled skillet, unzipping the bones in one cut of his knife.

"Good. I'm hungry," Adler said.

"You think you're hungry now," June said. "Wait until the end of the trip. You'll want to eat twenty-ounce porterhouse steaks, a dozen of them, baked potatoes floating in a bucket of melted butter, and a gallon tub of praline ice-cream."

In the middle of his first night, on his way to pee in the woods, Brooks peeked in through the mesh flap at June, asleep on her back. Her face was slack, and he felt guilty peering down at her, but couldn't help himself. She looked like a giant corpse in a soft-sided coffin.

Off in the dark, there were more stars overhead than he'd ever imagined. He saw a flittering shadow wobble from the woods into the other side of their camp. Kurt, in full camouflage, was walking in circles around the perimeter of their tents.

They got up at four thirty the next morning. In an hour, they were paddling through the layer of mist drifting over the water like a penitent cloud. That first full day of rowing, the water started easy, and Andrew had them practice rowing on his commands. Back-rowing. Push stroke. Sweep stroke. Cross draw. Double-oar turn. They moved positions to see how they would float better and silently faced the fact that the raft floated better with the three males on the opposite side of June. They spent the morning hours wan and listless. But by afternoon, there were times they fought forward, Brooks, Kurt, and Adler working furiously to keep even with the deep, powerful paddle strokes of June. Then, there were times when they ducked into the body of the raft to weigh it down as they passed over a violent stretch of rapids.

Toward the end of their first day rowing, Brooks spun sideways and dangled his feet over the side and watched the river's ribs pass below. His muscles ached with a dull pain radiating from his shoulders and throbbing down his lower back. He closed his eyes, tucked himself into a tight cannonball, dropped overboard, and drifted

137

downriver, the cold water easing his muscles, the vast blue sky easing something deeper and harder to name.

After setting up camp, eating by a campfire, and going to sleep early, Brooks was woken by the sound of Kurt's voice. "Andrew. Andrew. Andrew. Bear."

Adler leapt awake, and Brooks reached a hand out to hold him in place.

Andrew's tent zipper pulled back. There were a few heavy footfalls outside before Brooks saw Andrew's shadow with the rifle cut across the wall of his tent.

"HeeeYa. HeeeYa," Andrew was yelling. "HeeeYa. HeeeYa." Then the boom of a rifle shot, a quick crack, and stillness.

"Where?" Andrew asked. "HeeeYa. HeeeYa." He let out another shot, and the report split what was left of the night in half. "Do you see it?" he asked. "Kurt?"

Brooks felt Adler's hands grip his forearm.

After a moment of hearing Andrew running a circle around the fire, from tent to tent, he said, "All clear." Then, "Kurt. Where are you?"

As Brooks opened the tent and he and Adler stepped out, Andrew was walking toward June's bivy sack.

"June. You okay?" Andrew asked.

"Good Lord. I heard that thing snuffing around. Then it looked right down on me. It's a good thing it doesn't have a sweet tooth," she said and pressed her shaking palms into her hips.

A tree branch snapped behind them, and Andrew swung the muzzle to the woods, where Kurt, barefoot and in a pair of off-white tighty-whiteys, walked out of the trees.

"Look at this guy," Adler whispered to his dad.

"Where'd you go?" Andrew asked.

"Chased it off that way," he said and pointed a thumb over his shoulder.

"You chased a bear?" Adler asked.

"Maybe you should let the rifle shots scare them off next time," Andrew said.

"Next time?" Adler asked.

There was not a breath of air in the treetops.

"All this excitement is gonna give me a headache," June said.

"I'll get you some aspirin," Andrew said.

"Oh, honey. How about some horse doses of laudanum?"

Adler and Brooks restocked the fire, and Kurt walked the perimeter of the camp, aiming his flashlight deep into the woods to see if he could catch a glimpse of anything moving. "Shots scared it off," he said.

In their tent, Adler didn't lay down. He sat up on his sleeping bag. "I want to go home. I don't like this anymore."

"I know, it's scary now, but we can't stop or go back, buddy."

"No. We've been gone too long. Why do we have to be gone so long? I want to be back home, now."

"Ease back down, pal."

Brooks wanted to draw a clean sheet over his body and outlast the night. He slept uneasy and figured the others did too. They probably heard Adler wake up weeping several hours later.

In the morning, June hefted the poop bucket and carried it into the dark covering of evergreens singing a low melody that trailed behind her.

They set out in the gray false dawn. At first light, blue-black thunderheads were stacked over the ridge of the valley. By midmorning, a storm began pounding in from the distance. By the time they finished lunch, they were being drenched by cold, heavy rain that jumped up from the river as much as fell from the sky. The water drubbed their Gore-Tex jackets and pants and pooled at their feet all afternoon. The cold seeped down Brooks's neck and wrapped the bones of his back and then legs until he couldn't rid himself of the chill.

Adler's lips were blue, and his teeth were chattering. He was so tired and cold he set his paddle down and curled into a ball on the rubber lining of the raft like something washed up and fell asleep in the rain. The raft drifted on, and the boy, huddled in its heart, eased into his dreams. All but his father thought it was cute, when the boy started talking in his sleep. "It's not true. Not true." Mostly unintelligible words that Brooks knew held the traces of impossible longing.

"Teresa," Adler mumbled.

"The boy's got a girlfriend on his mind," Andrew whispered, smiling at Brooks.

"Sounds like it," Brooks said.

When the storm passed, they worked their way down another wide, easy stretch of water.

"What kind of work do you do, Kurt?" June asked.

"I've been an electrician and military contractor for my career."

"That's pretty cool," Andrew said.

Brooks's attention snapped to Kurt, a man who wandered the woods at night and chased grizzly bears in his underwear.

"What do you for the military?" Andrew asked.

"This last round was translations for intelligence work in Afghanistan," Kurt said, blurting it out like a confession. He lowered his head so he was looking at June's boots. From that angle, Brooks saw the deep circles of exhaustion under his eyes and recognized the burden of sleeplessness.

"What a weight to carry on those shoulders," June said.

"It can be. I have to think big," he said. "I had to translate these reports that decide the fate of other people."

Andrew let his fingers ply the surface of the river and watched for fish under the raft, but Brooks could see him stealing glimpses at June and Kurt.

June leaned forward and placed her hand on Kurt's knee. "It's good you've got some time to be away from that. That's too much for one man to carry by his lonesome."

The grand stretch of the river ahead was mother-of-pearl in the late afternoon shadows. All that driving on crooked highways that led Brooks and his son here seemed worth it as he watched the breeze take V shapes over the surface of the water. The clay riverbank was pocked with the paw prints of small animals like mink, otter, and fox, and deep pits left by hooves. There were old Indian names given to everything in these wild places. The old growth pine trees had absorbed those forgotten languages into the iron-hard centers of their trunks which now dripped in dense, green moss. Floating with the current, everyone quiet, admiring the tea-colored light, offered one sacred moment after another.

They drifted from the wooded runnel of the valley into an alluvial fan bordered by a great spread of boulder, gravel, and sediment from the river that shone in the full sun, breaking through the rain clouds like polished, golden stones.

The next day, Adler lifted his finger to the shore ahead of the raft. "Look." Off the bank was a gray wolf, tottering along the river, its coat already sheening toward autumn. It was moving away from them, but they all saw it, the grace it moved with, the deep sense of its belonging where it was, then the mystery of how fast it slipped into the heavier woods and was gone.

After a moment of silent reverence, Andrew leaned forward and slapped Adler on the shoulder. "Thatta boy. I've only seen one of those in all my years of doing this."

Adler was so excited, he cupped his hands around his mouth then and howled like a wolf, a sound that brought an upward thrust of joy over Brooks. Then Andrew joined in, and Kurt, then June. Their wild calls rose from the water and filled the trees. When their excitement went to his head, Brooks sent out his own raucous howl.

He had felt something during the darkest moments after his wife had died where he no longer trusted himself. He could see this sad transition locking his son's heart too, and he had to try everything to keep that from sticking. He wanted Adler to know these moments of life—spontaneous life—were out there to be had, that he could come find them in his own life whenever he was lost.

That night, Andrew had Adler set up a fire pit, circling stones from the river in the middle of the camp. Before dinner, Andrew led the group in yoga exercises on the shore, and they began making peculiar shapes of their bodies, creating an odd alphabet as they loosened their sore muscles. Between and during stretches Andrew sang a love song in Spanish that he sang to his daughter at her bedtime. The song started soft and sweet, then each note dipped and became layered with yearning. Brooks shut his eyes, twisted his spine, and was lost in the mournful, haunting serenade.

They ate their dinner, hung their food in bear bags, and chatted by the fire. The Milky Way mirrored the river, and the depthless stars flowed through the sky. Later, Adler woke up, sobbing. When Brooks tried to comfort him, again the boy woke without knowing he'd been dreaming, without recognizing the sadness still so close to him. In the early morning, the sun broke over the higher peaks and slid down to the valley like bloody yolk, and the wet rocks along the banks turned reds, russets, and blues in the light.

That afternoon, after floating downriver and resting, while Adler ran off into the woods to use the bathroom, Brooks and June sat next to each other on a log, eating peanut butter sandwiches.

"Why bring the boy?" June asked.

"I wanted him to get out into the natural world. It's a humbling feeling."

"I hear him crying at night."

After a moment, Brooks looked at June's expressive face. "We needed a change of scenery."

"I can understand that, you poor creatures. You boys need to let it all float away."

The next morning, Brooks woke stiff. Muscle. Sinew. Bone. Damp moss covered the ground. Dew covered everything. He and Adler each took two corners of their tent and shook the moisture away before stuffing it into the green nylon pack. The coming day was lovely, the sky blue. Over the crest of the mountain, the full summer sun warmed the vast range they were cutting through. Each limb of the Douglas Fir and Ponderosa Pine trees lining the water held patterns of light. This was so much better than the highway leading to his house back home, where the trees were full of tattered plastic bags that looked like gaunt, gray faces.

Adler had on an Australian digger's hat that hung from a leather strap around his neck. The sun drying their clothes heightened the stink of sweat. Unwashed armpits. Bad breath. Wet, moldering socks.

"Well, what a crowd of stinks we've got here," June said.

They spent the day rowing.

When they had set up their night's camp, eaten, and built the fire to a low roar, Brooks and Adler were the last to stay up. They were quiet between stretches of small talk. The boy's face was flushed and churchlike. Then his voice, thin as an eggshell, rose up in the darkness.

"Can I tell you about something, Dad?"

"Of course."

"You might get mad."

"Why don't you tell me and we'll see?"

"It's about something I did."

"Okay. Let's hear it."

Adler bit his lower lip. His teeth were square and white. "This one night after Mom died I heard the dog from a few houses down, Bailey is his name, barking its head off. I went out on the porch to see what he was barking at, but he was around the front of the house. So I walked to the sidewalk to see."

"What was wrong with him?"

"He was screeching because a big rat had him by the tail. Bailey's got this little wiry tail, and this rat was almost as big as the dog. It was pulling Bailey toward the gutter grate under the curb. Bailey's nails were scraping against the concrete."

"What'd you do?"

Adler peeled layers off a pinecone in his hands.

"I watched."

"You watched?"

"More than that too. I wanted to kick the dog in the gutter. I took a step forward to do it. I was going to help the rat. I don't know why." Adler cupped his hands together. His eyes fixed on the firelight. "When I really thought of what I was about to do I sort of snapped out of it. Then I jumped for a stick and started cracking it down on the rat until it let go and ran off."

Each coppery word his son spoke distilled in Brooks' ear. "That was brave."

"But Dad. I really wanted to rat to eat the dog. I don't know why. I don't know why I thought that."

"People think all sorts of things. Lots of sick thoughts. That doesn't mean you act on them. It doesn't make you bad or anything."

"Dad. After that I lay down on the grass and started crying. Like, I couldn't stop, and I don't think it was because I was sad for Bailey or scared I'd get caught."

Brooks remembered how he and Teresa never let Adler out of their sight. Years of worshiping everything he did. It occurred to him now that the only real shame of his own life would be that he would not be able to watch every minute of that brilliant scattering of Adler's time.

Adler was crying now. His face was damp in the firelight. The fire smoked as it ate into the wet wood, and Brooks thought perhaps he should find some story to begin sharing the recesses of his heart. He could tell him about Teresa. But he didn't. He couldn't. Every sentence he could utter about her had no end.

They went to their tent but stayed awake for a long time without talking and listened to the noise of wood-boring insects in the spruce trees.

After a while, Adler got up and went outside to use the bathroom. Brooks waited for him to come back and imagined his boy was off in the woods, crapping into a can or making some secret pact with God or trying to make sense of his life. There was no knowing his heart because it was so alone. The way all hearts are alone.

When Adler didn't come back, Brooks went to find him.

Adler was standing at the edge of the floodplain, next to a patch of gray wind cripples. Brooks stood a moment and watched his son's flat, hairless chest and veinless arms, so fragile and small against the craggy backdrop.

"Adler. You okay?

"Yeah."

"Can I do anything for you?"

"I don't know what's happening, Dad," Adler said. "Every time I think of—" He choked up.

"How about we say goodbye to her? It might help us get over some of these feelings," Brooks said. "We don't have to say goodbye just once. We can do it whenever we feel like we're holding onto too much."

Adler watched the ruddy water. His palms pushed into his eyes the way he did when he was tired as a baby. "Goodbye, Mom. You are my heart," he said.

Brooks felt his own heart thinning. He could see Teresa. Once so full of life that tiny arcs of milk sprung from her nursing-swelled nipples as she slept topless. Then he saw the sickness sapping her and the full weight of the last year, when grief passed in and out of everything, a fish living inside of him.

"We are never apart," Brooks said. "We love you every day."

Adler hid his face in the bend of his dad's arm. Brooks threaded his fingers through the hair on the back of his son's head. On one hand, this felt like something that needed to happen, but on the other hand Brooks wasn't so sure anymore. There was still no resolution. Nothing had been let go or solved. Nothing decided. There was no great shift in him or in Adler, though everything that had been a free float through his body—grief, fear, loneliness—seemed more a part of him now, consolidated, rather than lone invaders trying to pull him down. The pain was dulling as if it, too, had been drifting in the cold channel of the river.

"I'm going to go to sleep now," Adler said.

"Okay. I love you," Brooks said. In his mind, his son said he loved him too and something important unfolded. Clouds turned the water black. An owl flew over the trees and disappeared into the canopy. The scaled sides of fish rose in the moonlight to snatch at the surface. He let that imagined moment play out for a long time before going back to the tent.

On his way back, he looked down into the mesh flap of June's bivy sack and saw Andrew's braided ponytail and his pale white buttocks thrashing around on top of her. He looked away. Who was he to judge what arrangements people made in their lives? As he was about to zipper the flap of his own tent, he saw Kurt emerge from the stand of pine trees. His lean figure cut a fleet shadow. When he stepped into the clearing, the moonlight fell across his naked body and laid a soft glow on his mud-smeared chest and face.

When Brooks lay down next to Adler, the river was making its own music against the embankment. He still lacked the right words to confess his own feelings and unburden himself. He thought of laying out the emails he'd printed by the fire in front of everyone and saying, "Listen to these, will you please listen to these?" And if that didn't spark the words he needed to share that twin hammer strike of awe and loss he felt, he'd toss the papers in and burn them, pull out an ignited stick and write across the air in flame. He would speak to the wonder of his life, of these people's lives, of his son, of how spectacular and odd they each were.

UNBEND THE RIVER

The Year 1805

It was the height of summer when Silas came back from the river, out of the woods, and into the family fields. He saw what looked like a black thunderhead that was too close. It moved too fast. At the opposite edge of the field he heard it all at once. A dense black fog of grasshoppers burst from the sky and cascaded onto the crops. In minutes the fields shimmied like the skin of a great serpent. Silas hunkered to the earth until their short-horned, armored bodies blanketed him with a manic tree song that wormed deep into his head and leapt from his fingertips.

"Silas. Silas. Help me start a fire," His father, Jaren, yelled from the barn. "We'll smoke them out."

Jaren's voice yanked Silas free of a crippling sensation that the insects lifted him off the ground on their raw silk wings. He tried to concentrate. Gather and pile wood. Bring a smoldering log from the hearth. Blow on the kindling. Each step crushed grasshoppers, and he slipped on their soapy insides.

Jaren handed him two long willow boughs wadded with oil-soaked sheep fur to light in the new flame. In that moment Silas felt like his father was about to save their crop. Silas pulled the torches free and ran toward the edge of the field, but right away it was clear his efforts were insignificant. His fires useless. Grasshoppers flew through the burning wool, drifted off on flaming wings, and disappeared in the swarm.

His siblings, Juta, Harriet, and Darrell, screamed at the terrifying touch of so many insects, and the creatures perched on their tongues and edges of their eyes for moisture. Juta fell to her hands and knees and dug the insects from her throat with her dirty fingers.

Silas stood over her and waved the torches. He was fifteen years old. The swarm pelted his skin and cleared a path for an immense feeling of helplessness to enter. His family, and most of the neighboring farms, had poor crops for the last two years. No rain in the spring. Cold, dry winters. The wells were low. They'd spent the last of their resources to yield a crop—wheat—that for a time in the midsummer began to sprout with the rich green-and-gold-tasseled fringe of a full harvest. Now the swarm stripped away the wheat and swallowed the golden, russet, fully-bloomed leaves and buds of the trees, leaving only a pulsing dark wave that reflected the light off its million-backed thrust forward.

The grasshoppers flooded into their cabin and up the timber and river-rounded stone walls, covering nets of dried venison. Silas's mother, Zenobia, swatted at the walls with a horse-hair broom. Each stone she cleared filled in with the black shifting of more insects.

"They're destroying everything." She swatted the broom in front of her as she ran from their home.

Jaren dragged dried skins over the dye pits. The surface of the purple and red pits twisted with insects sinking into dyes. He took a dried skin, ran toward Silas, and snapped it out into the air so it fell flat over Juta.

"I'll get Harriet. You get Darrell."

Silas looked around but didn't see his younger brother. He searched the field until the tiny outline of the boy emerged from a gyrating black clot. Darrell was choking, and the sound added to the treacherous new noise of the world.

Throughout the day the insects writhed forward. Chickens pecked at the covered ground, gorging on the finger-length bugs until their stomachs burst. Silas imagined his stomach full of the churning mass of snapping wings and the whisper touch of endless legs jumping against his insides. He stopped in front of the bonfire to rest his hands on his knees and pray to whatever force sent the grasshoppers, asking it to call them back.

Throughout the night the furious snapping of wings grew even louder. Their dark bodies blotted out the sky. Embers sparked and drifted, hot orange stars against the animal darkness. The three youngest kids hid in the back of the cabin, under piles of skins where Zenobia wept over them.

"We're going to be fine," she said in penitent, dreadful sighs.

Silas heard her when he walked inside. He sat next to his siblings. He picked up Juta's tiny foot and squeezed it. A small squeeze so she knew he was there. He wanted to gather up all the skins and furs and stuff his whole family, his home, the fields, and the world beneath them to hold onto what little they still had.

By morning, when the insects had destroyed everything, the shrill, half-scream, half-plaintive cry of gulls hovering over the back part of the fields began.

Jaren pointed to the sky. "Another plague."

But the birds came upon the ruined wheat and began devouring the devourers. The sky became a deafening swirl of insects and birds colliding. Thousands of tireless gray-white birds. The gulls ate until full, went to drink at the river, vomited, and went to hunt again.

The gulls pushed the grasshoppers over the field, from east to west, from Silas's plot to the neighbors', and the swarm receded the way floodwaters seek out their previous borders. When the back end of a field had cleared, the soil was covered with crushed, stomped, burned, and spewed-out grasshoppers.

Bloated and dead seagulls and chickens lay scattered in the furrows.

"Gather all the dead chickens and birds," Zenobia said.

"Why?" Jaren asked.

"We can salt them. Eat them."

"You want us to scavenge?"

Zenobia squared her shoulders to him. "What choice is there? Gather the birds."

Silas watched as his father's shoulders slumped, and he got down on his knees. The bluntness about their impending hunger was a gut-punch truth that crumpled something weight-bearing.

"We're going to be fine," Zenobia said.

Silas walked to his stooped father to lift him back up.

"This isn't happening," Jaren said.

"Go get the birds," Zenobia said.

"There has to be something else we can do," but Jaren went out and began piling the dead birds.

Silas gathered baskets of the dead insects to soak in water, boil, and let the sun dry to be salted and stored for food, if needed, during the worst parts of the coming year. Zenobia hunted the field, pulled at the remaining crops, and dug down for the tuberous roots in a feeble attempt to salvage their total loss.

"I can't believe this," Jaren mumbled when he came back and saw his younger children sitting in a circle pulling feathers until their legs and laps were covered like filthy, molting birds. "We'll make this work for us. Something will work for us."

"I know," Silas said.

"I'll do something," Jaren said to himself now.

Silas knew his father, a tanner and farmer by trade, had lost his whole crop. The vegetable garden Zenobia used to feed the family had been chewed to a vegetal pulp. A bad year was coming. Another would lead to famine.

"We'll do everything we can. Do you understand, Silas? We'll find a way."

"Yes," Silas said, but he found no comfort in the words or the desperate ceremony of their repetition. The words felt false. Fill-ins for what he wanted to say. *Help. Help. Who cares from where. Help.*

Harriet reached over and tickled Juta with the end of a feather.

Jaren went to the dye pits and started ladling out the clumps of insects. He was tall, broad-shouldered, and flat-muscled, with coiled black hair over his pocked brow. His face was now gray and exhausted. His arms red up to the elbows from berries crushed in the pit. His eyes a startling cornflower blue.

Silas watched as his father held two fistfuls of goopy red insects and stared at them with a look of mystery and nausea as if he'd pulled them from his own body. Jaren squeezed his hands into tight fists, threw the gobs down and ground them into the earth with his foot.

"Okay." Jaren held his red dyed hands up to cover his face and stood like that without moving. "Okay."

Silas walked closer to his father. To comfort him. He took a large inhale. The inky smell of the dye pits stung the back of his throat. Jaren mumbled something to himself that Silas couldn't hear. He turned to his family. His eyes and cheeks red from his hands.

"I'm going to find work at the traveler's camp." He walked to the barn where he began to saddle a mean and hungry old mare to his wagon. The mare had thinned since spring and her ribs now showed.

"Can I come with you?" Silas asked.

"Me too," Darrell said.

"You stay here."

"I can help," Silas said.

"I know, but you stay here. Help your mother with the kids. Please. That's the end of it."

"What will you do?"

"Try to get work with one of the camps."

"Please, can I come?"

"Please, me too," Darrell said.

"No!" Jaren's voice was harsh. His face inked. He looked down at his sons. "It will be okay."

Jaren loaded his tools and supplies and set off to the path.

Silas watched his father's wagon rocking away.

"I'm going for more bugs," he told his mother and went out into the field. Among the rows he knew he'd have to cut back the dead stalks and plow them under. He liked to work and the feeling that he controlled what the fields produced. It was as much his work as his parents' that was destroyed. He got on his hands and knees and brought his face close to the soil to see all the bent legs, shelled husks, whisper-thin wings. The field was covered with hard insect bodies.

When his father's wagon turned the corner out of their property, Silas ducked into the woods. He stared at the last veins of chewed leaves. He stuffed several leaves into his mouth and tucked them into his cheek.

He walked fast for over an hour until he got to where the Allegheny River bends in a series of tight curves. At the start of the drought they brought buckets to water the garden, but it was too far to carry the full buckets. Too slow. Water sloshed out and onto the forest along the way so there was never enough for the plants. Now along the banks he searched for the exact spot the current touched closest to his lands. He imagined walking straight back from each curve, surveying where the land rose and rolled, dipped and vall-eyed. He'd find the straightest route to dig a trench to divert the river water. He imagined his family waking to him digging the last section of an irrigation channel through the valley that would save them from the dry growing season. A flood clearing the field. The astonishment on his father's face. His mother's arms reaching out to grab his siblings to hug them close. The water rushing over the fields and washing the insects away.

When he approached, the camp travelers leaving the hills set up to water the horses before moving into whatever it was they were looking for in Ohio. Along the river he went deeper into the woods so he could watch his father's wagon arrive. But he didn't see it come. Instead, he saw his father slip through the woods on foot. Jaren wore his deer hide hunting tunic, but he didn't have his bow. Slung over his shoulder was a leather pouch Jaren used to sprinkle powder around the barn and hovel to kill rats.

Silas followed at a distance. Knee-high clouds of last night's fog still floated over the dewy forest floor and when Jaren stopped, Silas lay down, and the wet white breath of the ground engulfed him. The shredded leaves caught no wind and were still. The pouch bounced up and down against Jaren's back as he walked. Silas kept low and slipped behind the trees the way his father taught him to do to stay hidden while hunting.

Jaren stopped north of the camp. The river wound wide and slow arcs through the whole region. It flowed to what Jaren said was an unknown land to the west once you hit Ohio, where Silas had never been. The river had been enough to imagine the rest of the world. He pictured himself picking up the rope of water and snapping it straight enough to see everything along the unknown banks, everything shifting through the woods, to unbend the river to see what fate rushed closer.

There had been no travelers for weeks, but as he trailed his father into the next bend in the river, he caught the sweet, charred scent of cooking meat. He snuck up through the trees. The camp was full. The first wave of travelers pitched sand-colored tents on the banks. In the fenced-in corral, tired horses nipped at each other with long, yellow teeth. Their roan hides, slick with dew, gleamed in the sun as they arched their long swan necks to eat moss and stray sprigs of clover. They shook their manes and shoulders to shrug flies, and their deep sighing, nickering, and whinnying carried through the trees. He saw campfires. Several friars cooked on one fire. The friars had black beards and wore brown robes cinched with white ropes tied in knots around their necks. A group of Wenrohronon guides sat around a different fire.

Two dozen horses filled the corral. Little ghosts of breath puffed free of their mouths. Jaren crouched low and snuck toward their watering trough. He pulled a fistful of white powder from his pouch, plunged his red stained arm in elbow deep and swirled the water.

Silas wanted to reach out through the woods to his father's wrist, grab hold, and wrench him back. But as quickly as he had snuck up on the horses, Jaren turned away. He stopped in the trees to rub his hand in the grass and scrub it with mulch. Then Jaren turned toward where Silas hid.

Silas dropped down even lower through the last thin wisps of fog. Only the river moved, all else in the world was still. On his stomach, he listened for his father moving away. The dirt and mulched leaves scratched at his skin—the feeling of insects covering everything again. He imagined crawling to the corral's watering tank and tipping it over, letting all the water his father stirred seep into the earth and away.

When he looked up again he didn't see his father. He got to his knees. Then a hand pushed him back into the dirt.

"Don't move," Jaren said.

Jaren lay down next to Silas. Jaren put his hands on the ground and his face into the dirt as though he were about to sleep.

"Don't move."

Silas stayed down in the dirt next to his father. They lay side by side until they heard the noises of the camp breaking down to depart. He imagined the friars by the camp. They spoke a different language. Each had weathered brown skin that pinched at the eyes.

"Franciscans. Years of traveling," Jaren said when Silas had asked about them. "It takes a toll."

Silas had always been interested in the travelers and the places they had gone to and come from. He had seen all manner of them so far. Men, women, and children. Their ages varied, but most were older and wore shabby clothes. There was one group dressed in fine, colorful clothes. Clothes dyed in pits like his father's. At night, when he was close to sleep, Silas saw himself easing his mud-caked clothes into the pits and lifting them out, splendid as those travelers.

The first time he snuck up to the camp one of the travelers in the group spotted him through the trees and made a hand signal to the others who all fell silent.

"We have a curious bird in the woods," they pointed to Silas. Silas was about to spring up and run when the man said, "Come talk with us little bird," and waved him over.

One of the men stood up and sat back down to make room for him by their fire.

Silas inched closer.

"Did you hear us telling stories?"

Silas nodded.

"Well come closer to hear better little bird."

Silas sat with the men, scared, but alert to every word. They spent the evening telling him stories of far-off places with crocodiles and hippopotami.

"He's a farm boy," another guide said. "Tell him about the wheat field where statues of gods poke out of the ground. Fists and crowns. Nothing else left."

He was still in his revelry when his father shook him.

"Come along. You may as well help me now."

They walked through the trees toward the road without speaking. The mare was still hitched to the wagon and tied to a tree. Rendering tools and a large bladder sewn from sheep stomachs and filled with water for the horse were stowed in the back. Jaren untied the horse and sat in the wagon without moving.

"We'll go after them. See if we can catch up." Jaren looked at Silas. "We're running out of options." The need in his voice unsettled Silas as the wagon rocked along the rutted path, beneath trees that were now bare well before fall. The wheels screeched because there was no animal fat to lube them with. Piles of horse and human excrement lined the way. From a distance Silas could tell the settlers had broken camp and left. Gray, ashen circles from fire pits lay around the riverbank.

"Now what?"

"We'll see."

Their horse crossed the river, plodding over the slick stones and dragged the rocking wagon up the opposite bank.

After an hour ride up the path, farther than Silas had ever gone, Jaren pointed ahead of them. "Look there."

Into the trees lay the mound of a roan horse. There were tracks on the dried trail from what looked like the wild stomping and circling of a horse. Silas studied the ground around the horse.

"Look at this," Silas said.

There was a large cleared puff of dirt where the horse and rider had fallen. The path they followed was a steady stream of prints in the dust going one way. Around the dead horse were the markings of a break in routine. A Wenro guide trying to calm the animal as it reared up before it fell. The long skid in the dirt from the rider pulled free by guides.

"What happened?"

"We'll see," Jaren said. He jumped down from the wagon and went to pull his tools from the back. Silas watched the story the dirt confessed and a feeling crept up the back of his neck. He studied the horse, stripped of its load, abandoned amid the markings of its last struggle. It wasn't an old horse. Not thin, either.

As if he could read Silas's face, Jaren said, "Maybe it had too many crickets in the belly?"

Jaren kneeled next to the horse, unfolded his leather satchel of carving tools, and pulled out his skinning knife. The first incision he made across the neck was deep enough to carve away at the fat tissue yet spilled no blood. Silas was amazed at how efficient his father was at working his knife lengthwise down the chest and stomach, curving his blade around the giant penis, and cutting to the base of the tail.

"Hold the leg up," Jaren said.

Silas held the horse's leg straight back by cupping both hands on the hoof. His father reached between the marbled pink muscle and the hide until his fists looked like living things tunneling inside the animal's body. Silas hadn't seen meat in almost a month and imagined the large flanks of horse over a fire, fat dripping and hissing on the ash, his family gorging on the haunches.

Silas hooked a rope to their wagon and knotted the other end around the horse's back leg. Jaren eased the wagon forward to roll it over so he could skin the other side and pull the hide free.

Jaren stripped away the entire hide in one piece leaving the fur around the horse's dirt-covered lips. He made easy work of the skinning. He used a handsaw to cut off the four hooves. The saw ground loose a fine, gray powder with each thrust. Specs of hoof dust sparkled in the slant light. Silas ran to the wagon and began gathering the tools to section the meat, trying to anticipate what his father needed. When he turned back, Jaren wiped the blade in the grass and packed away his tools.

"What are you doing?" Silas asked.

Jaren ran his hands back and forth over his chest.

"We need to carve the meat," Silas said.

"The meat's no good."

"What do you mean no good? We need it."

"Come on, son."

"Mom will want the meat. I want the meat."

"Not this one. Come on."

Silas studied his father as Jaren climbed into the wagon and patted the seat where he wanted Silas to join him. A thrumming unease burned through him. He looked at the skinned horse—red marbled, dirt smeared, grotesque. He imagined the white powder mixing into the water in the horse corral. That water coursing through the animals, seizing and locking up something in each of their bodies.

"Come on, son."

They went farther down the trail, away from their home and the dead horse. After several rutted turns through the woods Silas saw another prone horse and knew for sure. That shifting uncertainty that began to flower in his chest exploded into full panic. He squeezed his eyes shut.

His father was a good man—a good man who had done this foul thing.

When Silas felt his father's hand cup the back of his neck and give a gentle squeeze, his body went rigid.

"We'll do whatever is needed to take care of our family," Jaren said. "Family is everything."

The two stared at each other as the wagon approached the second dead horse.

"I wish you hadn't followed me but there's nothing to do about it now. We have to keep ourselves well. Your mother and the kids. You understand? We have to take care of them now."

Silas dwelled in the first rush of a wave of discontentment that was about to crash on him.

They cleaned the second horse, sawed off the hooves, loaded the hide, left the carcass for wolves and carrion birds, and went further down the pilgrim trail until they found the next circle of trampled dirt where another animal began to get sick. The third horse had its throat cut, a dreadful, unsteady gash mercifully thrust in after it fell and the rider could now guess its fate.

The Franciscans and their guides got more efficient at dispatching the next seven horses. The cuts across their throats became cleaner. They came earlier. The wild, stampeding circles in the dust turned into an agitated swaying. All the horses had dirt in their mouths. Silas pictured them scraping their teeth over the path, trying to dilute the sickness coursing through them.

"Most are pack animals," Jaren said.

Silas knew there was no knowing what the animals were used for. It was clear by the end of the day, before it got dark, that the tracks they followed now had men walking, and he didn't know if the friars could get on with their journey.

After working through the night they slept on the stinking skins in the back of the wagon. The stars were bright and low slung. They filled the sky. As a child, Silas remembered his father lifting him up at night and spinning him around so the stars blurred, streaked, and fell closer.

In the morning they returned home with a heap of furs in the wagon. The musk of large animals rose from the back with the incessant racket of flies.

Zenobia and Juta met the wagon at the barn. Juta's dirty bare feet danced off the ground as she waved to them, then she jumped and clung to the side of the moving wagon.

"There's so many," Juta called in her sing-song voice.

"Why not bring the meat?" Zenobia asked. Her huge, slightly slanting, hazel eyes locked on Jaren. Her luminous skin blushed up from her neck to her cheeks like a promise.

"The meat was bad."

"How bad?"

"Too bad to bring home."

"We can't eat the furs. You should have tried the meat. We could have tried."

"Zenobia. Stop. This is what we have."

"Not even a scrap?"

"It wasn't good, love. I'm sorry."

"We don't need good. What's wrong with you? Good is beyond us. Can't you see that? We'll take anything."

Silas's throat squeezed off the truth. A need to protect his mother from what happened emerged with a visceral animal want that surprised him.

Jaren ushered the wagon into the barn to unload the skins.

Silas and Darrell helped prepare the dying pits. Silas felt a vague pinch of fear as he began peeling horse furs off and stacking them at the pools. All summer settlers camped by the river. The guides would know not to camp there on their way back. They would pass word along or leave notes to the waves of travelers behind them about the campsite. They carved messages into trees for each other. Symbols that told of their passage. He imagined himself hunting the woods for those notes and scraping away the bark with his knife to make it look like a buck had rubbed it raw with its horns.

They soaked the giant horse skins in the round stone and mortar baths built for boiling and dying furs. The boiling tank was perched over a fire pit, and when the flame was stoked a broth of horse flesh and damp fur stifled the air. His father skimmed the fetid surface of the tank with a cup and tried to drink the foul soup but couldn't swallow it and spit it into the ground where the liquid soaked into the dry dirt.

"Can I try?" Silas asked.

"It's no good," Jaren said.

"I'm hungry enough to try."

Jaren was slow to share the cup, and near tears when he handed it over. Silas held the cup to his nose, pushed it away, then brought it back to take a sip. The rotten taste tightened the skin around his teeth before he had to spit it out too.

"Terrible, isn't it."

"Yes."

"Sorry son."

Once the skins boiled in the dye pits, Jaren added buckets of dried elderberries and beetroot shavings. He tossed in iron salt and mordant to keep the dyes fast.

"Why this color?" Silas asked.

"The treated hides bring a greater price." Merchants came along the river to the forges built by knife and blade makers. "The money from the hides will buy food and seeds for another planting. The money can save us."

"I see," Silas said.

He wished he hadn't followed his father. A good man. Though with the money from the horse furs would come new seeds to plant and grains which his mother could boil into a thick mush and flavor with wild fennel. If they could keep taking the hides perhaps the lost crop would not ruin them. Perhaps his father had found a way to save them—a dark toll on others overlaying their own salvation. He tried not to imagine what the Franciscans would do, how they would get to wherever they were headed.

They stirred with long poles until the lighter shades of horse fur bloomed into a deep crimson. Silas let his eyes blur and imagined he was using his pole to drown a red-brindled devil.

RED. OFF. RED. OFF.

Gene LaFall felt like he lived in three places. During the week, when he had to teach economics to undergrads at the Franciscan College, he stayed in a two-bedroom apartment in Olean where the second bedroom was made up with a bunk bed for visitors who never came. His second home was a rented studio apartment near his daughter's house in the suburbs of Cleveland three hours away. The studio had a bed, a recliner, and a television. He slept there on weekends so he could drive to his daughter's home to pick up her giant Newfoundland and take it to run in the state park woods. On those mornings his grandkids, the twins, would meet him at the door in their pajamas with happy screeching and hugs, still warm and smelling of sleep, sugar cereals, and syrup.

The dog was neglected, and though Gene had no great affinity for the animal, it would whine and jump in circles, nuzzling his palm with its wet nose until he leashed it and took it outside. But Gene lingered to get a hug from each of the kids. Make them do it all over again. He'd blow a kiss to his always-tired daughter. Her face drawn and hovering over a steaming cup of coffee she never invited him in to share because she had still not forgiven him for letting her mother down. Though this was enough. It was worth the extra rent payment that kept him living check to check because it kept him part of the kids' lives.

His third home, or what felt like his third home, was in the car, driving back and forth for the career that at some point broke off from his family life like a giant ice sheet and drifted away with him still on it.

The drive he knew by heart. The Southern Tier Highway, then a straight shot using Interstate 90. A refinery near Erie, Pennsylvania. Twin landfills rising out of the horizon. Flat fields. The monstrous state penitentiary outside of Cleveland. An agriculture college's black-heifer-and-sheep teaching farm. A seventy-mile stretch of windmills. He'd stopped in every gas station and rest stop. On one occasion he used every rest stop in one trip because of a stomach bug that sent him to the toilet and left him heaving between graffiti-coated stall doors that echoed the grotesque noises.

After finishing his Sunday walk with the dog, Gene was driving back to Olean, daydreaming about what he would do with the twins if they ever visited. Menu plans. Activities. Swimming at the student center. All the things his daughter had loved to do as a girl. Halfway through his drive, amid the windmills, he saw a horse trailer with shredded tires on the side of the road. A young man was on his hands and knees between the trailer and traffic looking to see what could be done with the spent rim.

Gene slowed down, eased onto the shoulder behind the trailer, and put his hazards on.

He had no idea how to change a tire on a trailer like that but knew there wasn't a gas station for thirty miles, and he loved moments like this. When the unexpected rose up and gave him something to do.

The man on his knees looked to be in his early thirties. A weight-lifter with yellowed skin, a blond ponytail, and half a dozen visible tattoos. One of a buffalo at the back of his neck. He hadn't shaved in a few days and wore the sketch of a black beard along his jawline. A horse's white tail swished across the back gate.

"Anything I can do to help?" Gene called as he walked closer.

The horse bucked and kicked the back door so hard the whole trailer shook. The man jumped and almost landed in the driving lane.

"Watch out," Gene said.

The man leapt back, his chest against the trailer to avoid whatever oncoming semi he must have perceived.

"Not a great spot," Gene said.

"No," the man said. "I ran over something that blew two tires on the truck and shredded the tires here. It spooked the horse pretty bad, too."

Gene looked up at the truck that had flat front and rear driver's-side tires.

The horse bucked again.

"So what can I do?"

"Well. I'm not really sure what to do."

"Got anyone to call?"

"Not that's close."

"Well. Nothing's close to here, I guess." The nearest gas station was a truck depot to the west.

An eighteen-wheeler flashed by, and the draft of wind flapped Gene's shirt. The white horse rocked back and forth and gave three kicks to the door.

"Easy. Easy in there," the man said. "Any ideas what I do here?"

"Can we call you a tow truck?"

"I have my own flatbed truck at home but I wouldn't know what to do with the horse then?"

"Can it stay in there?"

The man walked to the back of the trailer next to Gene.

"To be honest, I don't know. I'm just transferring it for my wife. It's pretty freaked out in there."

"Well. I can drive you to the next truck stop. They got an auto center with showers and the whole deal. Maybe they'll have a few spare tires or at least a donut to get you to a proper tire place. Probably near Dunkirk."

They left the horse in the lopsided trailer with a note tucked under the truck's windshield. Gene cleared his books on tape about astrology, mythology, and US history off the passenger seat to make room for the man, who introduced himself as Sugar Bergman.

"Where you taking the horse to?" Gene asked.

"My wife runs a farm near Olean. This horse was too wild for someone in Michigan, so I came out to get it for her."

"You a farmer?"

"I married a farmer's daughter."

"Alfalfa out in Olean, is it?"

"Some. Though it was nothing for a long time. Now my wife seems to make money from all sides. She plants soy and hay. Takes government subsidies. Has her own windfarm, which turned it around for us. Those bring in about twelve thousand dollars a year per tower. And we train horses."

"Sounds like an impressive woman."

"She is."

"So you work with her?"

"No. Well, sometimes. When I can't get other work."

"What's your specialty?"

"I'm a mechanic. But I worked at a seed store for a while. Then as a bartender at a place called The Tavern."

"I know the Tavern."

"I've had a lot of jobs."

"That's what you do when you're young," Gene said.

"Not that young."

"You're plenty young to me. I've got a daughter about your age. Just a kid. And the way I see it, if you've got at least another day ahead of you, you've got plenty of time to figure it out."

Gene pulled off the highway into Love's Truck Stop. The parking lot was full of multicolored tractor trailers parked side to side, ten across, and three deep. An obese woman in gray jogging pants and a sweatshirt was filling her tank by the diesel pump. She held a giant Super Gulp mug. Gene pulled to a stop.

"Let's look for what you need."

"You don't have to help me anymore."

"It's no problem. Gives me something to do."

Gene felt the small fleet of trucks vibrating on idle or waiting to fuel. Inside was a large convenience store, a hamburger restaurant, a truckers' lounge with pay-by-the-minute showers in the bathrooms, and an auto center where a person could by windshield wipers, wooden tire knockers, and snow chains. There was a laminated catalog of spare tires that were kept in the back room. One for the truck and one for the trailer would cost him three hundred and twenty-two dollars. And that would at least get him to a proper tire store where he'd have to pay for quality tires.

On the drive back to the horse trailer, Gene talked about all the semis in the parking lot.

"You'd be amazed. Each had such a random load of products from all over the world. Each gets produced, coded, shipped, transferred, stored, displayed, sold, used, reused, then scrapped and recycled in just about every corner of the planet."

"Seems like you know the whole system of how the world puts money to work."

"That's what I like about what I teach," Gene said. "My students have a hard time with the topic, but if they could just see it at work around them. How it isn't about money; it's about being busy and productive and can be a special thing to spend your time thinking about. So on the micro level, it's about what two tires do to your economy, but the macro is about what the cost of a barrel of oil in Toledo does to an alfalfa farmer's bottom line in Olean. The connections make this ever-expanding web. It always amazes me. Always reminds me to be interested in what I see."

"Including dumb-ass husbands stranded on the side of the road."

Gene laughed. "That's funny. I used to think the same thing of myself. Had a tough bastard of a father-in-law who made me never feel good enough for his daughter. He grew up during the Great Depression. Stern as all hell."

"He didn't think much of you?"

"Well. I thought that for a long time. He meant a lot to me, though. I'm sort of thankful he passed before my wife and I divorced. That would have been hard on him. It was hard on everyone."

It was past midday when they drove past the broken-down trailer, and Gene craned his head to see if the white horse was still in there.

At an emergency-vehicle-only U-turn on the highway, Gene pulled onto the gravel and waited for a gap in traffic to ease onto the southbound lane, then tracked back to where he'd parked earlier behind the trailer.

Gene stayed to help Sugar. Through the air slats in the trailer he saw the horse was frothed in sweat. Its nostrils flared with each breath. Its ears were pinned back. When it sensed Gene it kicked at the door.

"I can't change the tire with her in there," Sugar said.

"Doesn't seem like a good idea," Gene agreed.

Gene rolled the spare for the trailer from his car. It was meant for a boat trailer but would work.

Each truck that passed made a deep sucking sound that felt like an ear popping.

Sugar had the truck's jack laid next to the trailer. "How am I going to do this?"

"Will the horse come out kicking like that?" Gene asked.

"I don't really know this horse. It could kick me into that field, for all I know." He gave Gene the nervous smile of someone about to try something that scared the shit out of him. A look Gene knew from the mirror. From memories of his own life. Moments like this.

Gene opened his passenger-side door and stood behind it, ready to hop in if necessary.

Sugar held a rope lead in one hand and eased the trailer's door bolt up and back.

"Easy, girl," he said, and cracked the door open. "Easy."

The horse kicked the door open, and quick as fox, Sugar stepped into the stall next to the horse and looped the lead around her neck. In a moment he had her backing out of the trailer, taking a big step onto the road in front of Gene's car.

The horse reared her head and shook it, but Sugar tugged her to the side, and the horse stopped in the culvert and took a tremendous yellow piss. When the horse was done, Sugar walked it up to the front of the trailer and tied it to an eye bolt in the cab of his truck.

"Nice work," Gene said.

"Lucky not to have taken a horseshoe to the head."

Gene took a white button-down shirt from his overnight bag, walked behind his car, and waved it to steer oncoming vehicles to the other lane to avoid where Sugar was propping up the trailer. Several cars slowed. Some changed lanes and whooshed past.

Gene looked back to see Sugar on his hands and knees the same way he'd found him earlier in the day. Now he was cranking on the crowbar to loosen the bolt. His hands slipped, and his knuckles punched the ground. Gene had done that before. He could envision the dark scabs across the top of his hand.

Gene went back to waving his shirt so Sugar wouldn't catch him watching. After a moment, Gene looked back at the trailer and saw the horse run in front of the truck and into the road. It crossed both lanes, into the trough of the median, and up the other side at a full gallop, where it shot in front of an oncoming semi. The semi blared its horn.

Sugar looked in time to see the horse just miss getting slammed. When the semi passed the horse had already jumped the wire fence on the far side of the highway and was galloping across the field toward the endless rows of windmills.

Sugar called the local police and told them what had happened. Where he was and what the horse looked like.

Gene drove to the closest exit and doubled back, this time taking the northbound frontage road, and when they saw the truck and trailer, still tilted to the concrete, he took a dirt road east toward the windmills where the horse had run.

Sugar held the halter and lead in his lap. He tugged at the rope and ran his thumbs over the coarse fibers.

"I'm sorry I've wasting your whole day," he told Gene.

"Don't sweat it. You know those little old ladies that wander the grocery store all day? Consider this my grocery store and my wandering. Something to do."

"Nice of you. Not many would stop." Sugar tugged the lead again. "I didn't tie this tight enough. I'm such an idiot."

Gene had papers to grade. He'd ignored them all weekend. He'd planned on grading them tonight before bed, but it was beginning to get dark. It didn't bother him, though. A few more days without their C and D papers wouldn't kill any eighteen-year-olds.

The windmills blinked on and off like a long runway's landing strip. This was the way of the future. The human future always followed the flow of energy. Wind. Sun. Water. Oil. Coal. Lumber. Back to pieces of shale sparking together over kindling to start the first flame.

He liked the strange-looking young man next to him. He was honest with how he felt. His own son-in-law was always a low flame toward him. Polite but distant. It set the measure of how his daughter and the twins interacted with him or how they avoided him altogether. Sugar seemed more to-the-point. Like he was trying his best and knew when he wasn't up to it.

He drove slowly. Gravel ticked against the undercarriage. They saw no sign of the horse. Once, on a summer vacation during graduate school, on a trip to Glacier National Park in Montana, Gene had seen a dead horse swollen on the side of the road. The extended barrel of its belly about to burst. Stiff legs tilted like bent fence posts.

"You know, when the Berlin Wall came down, all these geniuses in my field of study from Eastern Bloc countries flooded into the

United States. Every big university gobbled these guys up and gave them plum teaching jobs. They had Nobel Prizes. Were world famous. Big thinkers. It made it impossible for me to ever leave the dinky school I teach at. For a long time I kept trying to get a job closer to home in Cleveland. I knew it was a strain on my family. But I kept trying. Of course, you can guess it never worked out."

Sugar grinned and looked over to acknowledge he'd heard, then he went back to scanning the horizon.

"For a long time I felt that letdown was something my wife and in-laws saw as a failure on my part. I was so freaked out about not being good enough I projected that everyone else was judging me for that. I think it shot my confidence. I would get in the car and do this six-hour drive to work and back to Cleveland with this mantra of self-flagellation."

The lights on the windmill were synced. Red. Off. Red. Off. Red. Off. Like a path to some crystal future. Soon it would be dark, and there would be no finding the horse.

"I got wrapped up in the thought that I was failing, and it made me mean for a while." He looked over at Sugar. "I hope I'm not talking your ear off."

"No. It's fine."

"Don't worry. I'm searching, too."

Sugar nodded.

"My in-laws were at our house for a Fourth of July weekend. My father-in-law spent the whole time doing a puzzle with my daughter on the porch, and I was trying to deal with this great big infestation of moles I had in my front yard. Dozens of them had burrowed all over, and everywhere you stepped the ground would pock in, and you'd fall and twist an ankle. It wasn't safe, so I was trying to get rid of them. I ran a hose down there and flooded them out. But that didn't work. I threw little poison pellets down the holes. I packed the holes with dirt. I even tried quikrete. It was comical I guess, but I kept getting madder and madder, because he was there watching me not do what I was setting out to do. All weekend I kept feeling like a fool, and the more embarrassed and angrier I got the stupider my plans became. By the time he'd left at the end of the weekend I was beside myself, and the moles were still there."

"Can we take this turn here?" Sugar said.

Gene turned left heading north down a road that had windmills on both sides.

"I'm not even sure what we'll do with her if we catch her," Sugar said.

Gene drove and kept talking. "Years later, my father-in-law told me he liked watching me fight those moles. I thought, you son of a bitch. And you know, I think he sensed my anger. 'Probably not the way you think, though,' he told me. 'I liked it because it was clear you wouldn't give up on a god damn thing. You'll belabor it to death. Stubborn or shamed, doesn't matter, you'd keep trying even when you felt like an idiot. That was when I was most proud of you. Proud that my daughter found a man like that. That's what it takes to love another person in this world.'"

Gene looked over at Sugar. He could still see his father-in-law as he was then. Gray-faced and weary but still upright, and everything he said felt earned. When he told Gene that it felt like a gift.

"You never know what others judge you by," Gene said. "Your wife will understand this."

The field was too big. It was getting dark. The horse would be spooked by the gusts from the windmills and keep running.

"We probably won't find this horse," Sugar said.

"Probably not."

"Can we keep looking?" Sugar asked.

"Of course."

Gene could imagine the feeling of the half-crazed horse at the base of the windmills tracking across the plains. Running aimlessly from one place to the next. He'd been doing it for years. He drove up every weekend to walk a slobbering beast through the woods, to be steady, to grind away at the hurts that created rifts between the ones he loved. Grinding away was all he had to offer now.

THE THOUSANDTH DAUGHTER

On the shuttle bus between the terminal and parking lot my wife Tillie starts talking to the odd-looking young couple.

Tillie and I married three years ago. She can't help but talk to everyone; her friendliness and warm voice are a silver rope she pulls people close with. I know this. This is what she used on me, cradling me from extreme loneliness.

"We took a little trip for my birthday," Tillie says to them. "Went to play some bingo."

"Oh, is this your birthday?" the young woman asks. The girl, in her early twenties, dyed black hair to the middle of her back, dark eyeliner around her captivating dusty green eyes, black lipstick, wears thick-soled leather boots and a black dress printed with a big rubber duck on the chest. Despite this vampire look, she's pretty in the spark of the overhead running lights.

"Tomorrow," Tillie says.

"Mine too," the girl says.

"No kidding." Tillie folds her arms on the stretch of denim under the heft of her breast.

"I'm now Medicare age. Can't believe it."

"Our young ladies share the same birthday," I say to the slumped-over, muscular young man with pumped-up biceps, a buzz cut, copper-colored chin beard, wearing a faded Buffalo Sabres jersey. His eyes are like pits filled with dark liquid.

"Looks like it," he says. A carrot-sized hole runs along the crotch of his jeans. He's wearing pointy snakeskin boots with scales flaked off at the toes.

"Is there any skill to bingo?" the girl asks.

"No," Tillie says. "But it keeps us old timers doing something. We were just in Reno, but we've now played in sixteen states and on the islands of San Juan and St. Thomas." Her moon-face is all smiling teeth and contentedness with our life. "And where are you two coming from?" Tillie's voice is a cheerful birdsong.

"We're from upstate New York. A place called Olean," the girl says. The boy says nothing. He's looking at Tillie. Tillie packed into her wide-bottomed jeans, her gray hair put into a bun for travel.

"Do you live there or here?"

"We're going to try to make it out here for a while," the girl says.

"How's the fire been?" the young man asks and points out the windows where the last of the light to the northwest carries pillars of smoke from the fires eating away swaths of dead trees killed off by the pine beetles.

"Not good. The news says the fire northwest of Fort Collins, where we live, reached fifty thousand acres over the weekend. They say if it moves south to the I-70 corridor with all those dead trees that the blaze will be visible from space."

Despite the fires I'm happy to be going home. The traveling is something Tillie loves, but I love coming home. Tillie reaches out from her seat and places a hand on my knee. Her middle finger rubs over the raised scar from my knee replacement.

"Well, bingo seems like a cool reason to go seeing the country," the girl says.

"It sure is," Tillie says.

The girl looks back out the bus window at the vertical swooping white tent tops of the Denver terminal made like the giant sails of a prairie schooner. The bus lurches and the girl jumps an inch out of her seat, and her hands snap to her side.

"You okay?" the boy whispers.

She shakes her head.

"Oh," Tillie says. "Are you two expecting?" her smile reaches out to them in the half dark.

I'm embarrassed by her frankness always piercing any sense of decorum I've put up over a lifetime.

The girl puts her hand over the boy's and pulls it to her stomach. "Yes," she says.

The boy's eyes dart to her like this is news to him.

"Oh, I'm sorry for prying," Tillie says. "But very exciting. What a blessing for you two."

"Thank you," the girl says. The boy tries to pull his hand away, but she holds it. "Yes. It is."

"So nice," Tillie says. "Do you have family here?"

"No. We're going up to Fort Collins too," the girl says.

"Well, we'd be happy to take you two up there if you need a ride," Tillie says.

I stare hard into the side of her head to make it clear I want no part of this, but she ignores me.

"Be no trouble at all for us and save you money on a rental," she says.

"Wow. We could use a ride up there," the girl says.

Tillie motor mouths through the parking lot with Gothic Duck and Zombie Eyes, whose real names are Nedra and Dax. On the first half of our drive west and north along the Front Range, she talks about bingo and our farm house with the cabin by the stream. She tells them how I retired seven years earlier from Kodak. Started as an engineer in their Rochester office. Moved to Colorado with the company twenty years ago. Took over a research and development lab that was responsible for moving from film to digital pictures. It was in Fort Collins I did my best work. She tells them all this but not that it was here I lost my first wife, Martha, to what turned out not to be a cyst. I retired to spend more time with her and also because Kodak began talking about sending pictures straight from the camera to the internet—a young man's game, beyond me.

Then Martha passed and I spent three years with full days alone and no work.

Work allowed for a shutting off from the world. Martha allowed a structure to my life. When I no longer had either of those, I went to a legion hall bingo night to be around other people where I sat next to Tillie. I fell into her to fill the void and accepted whatever life she wanted for me, so I wouldn't have to craft my own. I was a moth. Martha was a light. The light went out and I fluttered in darkness. Tillie was a new light. Tillie with her stout weight and incessant chatter filled a void that terrified me. Tillie with her bingo, which I went along for, until I began to enjoy myself. A simple game to keep busy and travel. The travel keeps something on the books to look forward to. I think something to look forward to is important. It keeps hope a constant part of one's life. And, Tillie needs the strangers to talk to. She's never said this, but it's true. Same way I never said that fear of loneliness brought us together.

Along the drive, the air begins to take on a thicker gray smell like dense wood smoke.

"So, where is it in Fort Collins you'd like to go?" I ask.

"Maybe a motel by the highway. One not too expensive," Dax says.

"You kids don't have a place to stay?" Tillie asks.

"A motel will be fine," Dax says.

"No, no. We can do better than that for you." Tillie cups the back of my hand as I drive. The smoke makes a wide gray ribbon over the mountains.

"Well," I say, but Tillie cuts back in.

"We've got a little one-bedroom cabin on our property we'd be happy for you to stay over in."

"A good place to spend the night. Just the night," I say.

"Oh, stop, you." Tillie pinches my arm.

Our home is on eighteen acres of rolling land before the foothills rise up as a buffer to the full shock of the Rockies. It's a middle ground, not domesticated, not all the way wild. There's a Great Pyrenees a few properties down that lumbers out of the foothills dragging coyotes in its jaws. Its nose is a patchwork of raised black scars. Along the stream shooting off the Cache la Poudre River there's a pack of dirt-field mutts that go howling around their horse pastures and wind cripple orchards, chasing after anything that moves. Scary at first. Raise that primal part of the body, hair on end, spring in legs, hands into fists.

A neighboring lot rents one of its outbuildings to a Mexican family. I'd gotten their mail on accident once and went to deliver it for an excuse to be around someone. I tried talking to this old lady on the porch after handing over the letters, but she didn't speak any

English. Out of the corner of my eye, I saw her little kitten walking the top of the split-rail fence. I looked because I must have seen the shadow swoop down. This giant bird, some kind of eagle or huge owl, snatched the kitten. Silent. That kitten was limp as soon as the talons dug in. The bird didn't even flap its wings but glided right over the kitten and away. I tried to tell the lady what had happened, but with the language barrier, there was no getting that across. It was a futile feeling needing to tell her something but not being able to communicate. At the same time I was feeling down about that lady's cat, I was in total awe of the shadow that carried it away.

In the morning after our car ride with the young strangers half a dozen helicopters with huge buckets suspended from cables fly to and from Horsetooth Reservoir dipping up water to douse the blazes. The helicopters seem to come from everywhere and buzz over the small cabin the kids spent the night in. People up the canyon are losing their homes. If the fire keeps spreading my property will be in danger.

Tillie rolls toward me as I leave the room.

"Get the young lady a birthday card from us, will you?"

"Yes, dear," I say.

After drinking my coffee, some time reading, and packing my gym bag, I leave a birthday note and a small present for Tillie—a picture album with photos of us on each of our trips, the names of the state or territory printed on each page.

In town, emergency vehicles are everywhere. A crew of smoke jumpers is set up in the park after a trip into the heart of the blaze. The local paper said many of the fire crews are Blackfoot and Spokane Indians flown in to help. They look like ash-covered miners. Veins the size of garter snakes uncoil from their wrists up to their shoulders. I've read books about men like this and the free fall they take into burning forests. They're in top physical condition. They pack in gallons of water. I watch them rest in the park and long for such youth again.

Tillie is sitting on the couch doing a crossword puzzle when I get home.

"Did you find a card?"

I give her the postcard I found at a gas station that says, *Fort Collins is calling.*

She looks at the card. "Not a great effort on your part."

I shrug and walk to the window. "You think they're going to sleep the day away?"

"Well, why don't you go knock on their door and ask if they're hungry?"

I walk out the backdoor and down the dirt path to the cabin. I'm not halfway to the cabin door when I hear the girl make a wild keening sound inside. I freeze listening to this. Unsure of what to do or exactly what I'm hearing.

Hours later, while I'm prepping Tillie's birthday dinner in the kitchen, Nedra emerges from the cabin. Dax follows. He's slung over and apelike. She takes a running step toward the stream, an offshoot of the Cache La Poudre River that has made the property value triple since I bought it, and will make it triple again when everyone in the west realizes they're running out of water. It was too dark when Tillie led them to the cabin last night and the girl is surprised by it now. In the water, her hand jumps to her side again as it did on the bus the night before.

"They're alive," I yell to Tillie in the other room.

"Well, make a lot of food. I bet they've got an appetite." She giggles. I told her what I heard. "Don't be such an old prude," she teased when I tried telling her it was more than love noises.

Dax kicks off his boots and steps a pale white foot into the water, then pulls it out. The water is freezing. Dax tries again, this time getting ankle deep. He walks in up to his knees. I go back to chopping vegetables. Nedra's voice blows in.

She's standing knee-deep and lifts the hem of her shirt over her shoulders and peels it over her head. Her bra is yellow, her skin white. She plunges her shirt into the water and presses it against a large cut above her hip. I lean closer to the window. Smaller lines crisscross the tops of her arms and ribs like a wild cat clawed her to pieces. The shadow of older marks notch their way up her legs and arms.

"Tillie, come here," I yell.

"I'm in the bathroom."

Dax is deeper now, lifting cups of water with his hands to his armpits and chest, the back of his neck and face. A colorful smear of a tattoo rolls from his right shoulder to his back. He splashes Nedra with a slow arch of his hand.

I go to the bathroom door and knock. "Come out, now."

"Hold on. Hold on."

Tillie comes out wiping her hands on a green towel. I lead her to the window but the kids are no longer outside, and the cabin door is closed.

"That girl's all cut up," I say.

"What?" she says.

"She's got a slash on her side. Like a stab wound."

"A tattoo."

"She's covered in cuts."

Tillie turns and keeps looking out the window at the cabin.

A bomb's gone off in my chest. A bone-deep heat rises in me.

A flash of panic of not knowing what is happening with this girl gives way to anger that I am surrounded by strangers, in and out of my home. Or worse, that I've become the stranger.

Tillie sets the table for four and goes out herself this time for the kids. A few minutes later they are all walking into the house.

"Come on in. Sit. Sit," Tillie says.

"Thank you," Nedra says. Dax stands at the door as if unsure of how to enter a house. "Come on, Dax."

When the boy sits down, Tillie starts in on them.

"So, you guys must be tired from your travels."

"Yes. Sorry we slept all day in your cabin," Nedra says.

"Pregnancy can be hard." Tillie hands a salad bowl around the table. "So, what are your plans out here?"

"Dax is going to try to find work on a ranch. Or an oil rig job in Laramie."

"Any leads?" I ask.

"Heard of some," Dax says.

"Well, Maybe I can have Randy drive you up there, Dax, to see if something good will come along. Nedra can rest here," Tillie says.

I serve them green beans from the garden, pulled pork from the slow cooker, and fresh cuts of French bread. Nedra smiles with what I take to be a put-on smile. Dax is shoveling food into his mouth. I'm still tense from the electric shock of the girl's skin.

We eat, and Tillie starts asking trivial, safe questions. Nedra answers. I can tell Tillie is happy young people are in the house. She gets up, serves more food, and touches Nedra's back as she sits down.

It's strange to have a full table. Martha and I could not have children. Tillie, who wanted a dozen, settled for a career teaching. Thinking of both my wives because of these strangers, measuring our lives against the possibility of youth, makes me more irritable.

"What do you do for a living?" Nedra asks.

"Oh. I was a school teacher."

"What'd you teach?

"Home economics."

"To what ages?" Nedra asks.

"High school girls, mostly," Tillie says. "I liked being with those girls at that age when everyone else finds them ungovernable."

"That must have been fun," Nedra says.

"It was, and some of them keep in touch," Tillie says. She's excited to talk about her girls. She calls them *her* girls. "Most don't, but that's okay. I was part of their lives, and they're still part of mine. Like I've got almost a thousand daughters walking around the state of Colorado."

"Tell them how you got fired," I say.

Tillie looks at me like she's realized she had no idea before this moment who I was. It may be true, too. I've been on my best behavior with her. Hiding away most of what I think for comfort's sake. Over my life, there have been very few moments I revealed myself. To Martha. To Tillie. Now I see, even to myself. This is how I've emerged as this crusty old man with out-of-whack feelings. It's odd; I thought that after all this time, when a life has taken its size and shape, such a great clarity would no longer lie in dormant, secret places inside of a person. I had hoped getting old would allow some octopus free range over my mind, ink-blotting out my own uncertainty, one splatter after another.

Tillie takes a deep breath and looks from me to the girl.

"I taught classes on raising kids but it sort of fell out of favor and off the curriculum, so I retired early. Not fired. Right Randy?"

"Sure," I say.

This is the first time I've betrayed Tillie. She told me about the fake babies, but I've never heard her tell anyone else about them. Tillie takes a deep breath, then looks from me to the girl, blindsided by my rudeness.

She had taught a class on raising kids and ordered these state-of-the-art dolls that cried and went to the bathroom. They were meant to drop a baby into these girls' laps, so they wouldn't go out and have their own too soon.

Her little school was on the western slope. That all happened before I met Tillie. I had often thought of those babies, though. Tillie had distributed them, and she'd seen a girl walking down the street, cradling the child, giving it a bottle. From a distance it looked real, and she felt pangs of jealousy and hope for those girls who would go on to have their own families.

The parents were furious. When it got into the local papers, every crackpot in the mountains started writing Tillie. She could still quote the worst. Mostly misplaced rage that Tillie was encouraging young girls to be sexually active.

Tillie had not thought twice about the giving the girls the dolls. Most of the girls didn't either. The storm was harsh and came hard at her, but she weathered it. Then one of the girls took her doll in a backpack on a weekend camping trip and lost the whole pack when a canoe flipped. The little baby drifted off in the deepest channels of a mountain river.

When Tillie didn't replace the doll, saying she wanted to let the girl feel the hurt, the school board got involved.

I asked her why she said this. Why she thought it?

She told me she believed dealing with feelings head on and accepting them as part of your life in the present will lessen the weight of those feelings throughout the rest of your life. At the time it felt to me like a non-answer, though it has eaten at me since.

That there would be this unknowable facet of her character I could not fathom, and that she may have spoken so clearly of part of my behaviors I'd been blind to.

The math teacher in her school, whom I never met but will always like for being cold about the whole situation, said, "It's a good thing to have happened. It will teach them about probability. How mistakes and accidents will fall upon their lives."

Maybe it is thinking of the math teacher's probabilities that makes me raise my finger, point to Nedra's side, and blurt out, "I saw that slash on your side."

Tillie slaps the table hard.

Nedra's hand rises to touch her side and her face drains of color.

"An accident," Dax says.

Silence sits like a noxious stranger between us. I start to replay everything they've said to us so far to see what may be true. The same birthday. The pregnancy. A reason to come to Fort Collins after we told them where we live.

Tillie's eyes are blazing into the side of my face so I won't ask any follow-up questions.

Nedra stands up. "Well. Thank you for letting us stay the night and for the food." She walks toward the door.

"This was our pleasure," Tillie says. "Forget about my grumpy husband. He's tired from traveling, too."

"Yes," I say, shrinking from the sidelong glare Tillie is shooting me.

"You two must be as well. Travel is stressful. You're welcome to relax in the cabin another night if you like. We'll take you to town anytime."

The kids look at each other. Their own silent messages.

I leave the room. I can't explain how awful it was to see the girl covered in scars. Their obvious need bothers me. Not because I don't want to help them, but because it makes me feel like I've missed out on a lifetime of helping and connecting with others, of being some part of a larger human circle. Martha pushed me to excel at work, work done in offices and labs, not around the young, wandering, and lost, who Tillie must have cradled in her heart in those classrooms before sending out into the world. Her need to tend to Nedra and Dax is foreign to me and shines a light on how much more open to the world Tillie has always been.

The kids walk out to the cabin. Tillie is standing in the doorway looking at me.

"That girl belongs in a battered women's shelter," I say.

"Well. Maybe. Maybe it's something else," she says.

"What else?"

"Well. Maybe where they are from kids raise up rough is all. And these girls sometimes have little seeds inside them that grow nasty vines. It's not easy to see why they were planted and how they grow, but it's a delicate business. One that isn't so easy to jump on and label. It takes a bit of patience to get at."

"Well, it's awful."

"I can tell. But you'll get over it. They've decided to stay another night."

"Well, they almost slept from night to night so no surprise."

"Behave, and be kind," she snaps. "This isn't the Randy I know."

That phrase pings a nerve. The way I've acted tonight is closer to the Randy I know myself to be.

Tillie lets me alone in the den to read for an hour. It gets dark outside. The first stars wink through the smoke. I'm reading a biography of Lyndon Johnson. A pragmatic man I can appreciate. Martha wrote notes to me in the margins of my books when she knew she was dying. She scribbled little memories of our lives together on random pages.

I never scan ahead to look for them as I want her tight scroll to be a surprise. When I go several books at a time with no secret message from her I grow nervous, but so far, there've always been more notes to find. Tillie has yet to pick up a book from my shelf so the notes from Martha have stayed my secret.

Tillie calls me from the other room.

"Let's drive out to the road over the reservoir."

"Why?"

"The radio says people are going up there to see the fires."

"The fire is coming closer to us. Why would we want to go closer to it?"

"Come on. It will give us something to do. The reservoir road is high up enough to see into the mountains."

"Okay," I say. Though I don't want to go.

"Good. We'll take the truck and you can go ask if our guests want to go for a ride."

"Well, wait a minute."

"Get out there with you. Go on," she says, and like a scolded mutt I trudge out the backdoor, down the path, uncertain of what odd love ritual I will overhear or interrupt.

"Hi," Nedra says as she opens the door. Her voice is quick. She's putting on a false face. We have that in common.

"Would you like to go for a drive up the ridge with us?"

"Sure," Nedra says with no trace of the anger I must have caused her over dinner. The two of them follow me out to my old DeSoto flatbed.

Tillie is standing by the door with a paper bag full of drinks and slices of a birthday cake in Tupperware squares.

"You kids can have some snacks as we drive," she says, handing the bag over.

Along the city roads the dense clouds of smoke around the streetlights make little yellow skirts of light that dance overhead as we pass beneath. We drive up to the reservoir.

"This air can't be good for them back there," Tillie says.

"Bad for her baby," I say, the last dredges of crankiness spewing loose.

"Well. After tonight, I think that girl is about as pregnant as I am," she says.

The kids' heads bob through the rear view mirror. I'm a bit shocked by how dull we've been with them, how we've believed anything they'd said.

"Do you think it is her birthday too? Didn't they say they were going to Fort Collins after we mentioned the spare cabin?"

"Maybe," she says. "And maybe you can take him for a day away job searching so I can get some time with her alone."

Each of the kids has a hand on the gunnel of the truck. Once I stop the truck they stand and point into the distance and hold hands.

Many other cars are driving the hills to peer back into the mountains. The contours of the western hills are traced by a glow red as magma. It's terrifying how close the flames are. Wood smoke chokes the air and sinks into the fabric of our clothes.

I make to get out on the ridge but Tillie grabs my hand. She's smiling at me. With the exception of my being rude to her earlier, she's been smiling since we met the kids on the bus.

"Thank you for bringing us here," she says.

The way she says *us*, like it's familiar and includes the four of us comes easy to her. I sit back and watch the red outline of the kids standing in the back.

"I don't understand these two," I say.

"We don't need to. We just need to be kind to them and see if we can help as they pass along." She pulls my hand into her lap. Out her window, far below, is Horsetooth Reservoir. I try to sit easy in the truck and be content watching the world outside the window.

But I'm not easy. I feel a stabbing pain knowing that at some point my old life and wants submerged, and even Martha became a quiet ache in the back of my mind. At random times I'd surprise myself picturing Martha walking the property, past the wind cripples, over the river-smoothed stones, her fingertips reaching out to graze the white fists of bear grass in bloom as she walks toward me. I can shut my eyes now and see her shape staring out over the reservoir. What would Martha think of my bingo games? Of Tillie? Of Tillie's one thousandth daughter in the bed of the truck? What would Martha think of my handing my life over to Tillie?

Tillie lets my hand go and takes out her camera. A Kodak I bought for her last birthday. I worked on its predecessor, laboring for years and decades in a lab. The fruits of my labor must have captured an endless stream of shaky, disconnected moments of a life, a million strangers' lives. I worked so others could hold onto pictures of who they had been as they free fell into the pulsing center of their own lives.

The air is throbbing with helicopters dipping water. People call to each other from where they sit on the hoods of their cars or on rocks. Their leashed dogs bark and bay. They watch the river of fire burn over the ridge line. Ash travels on the high breeze. The subtle anger of today has opened a hairline crack in me, and I feel meaningfully alive to myself and to others for the first time since Martha left me, but instead of being calm, or joyous, I feel an unbearable anxiousness.

Behind me is the young couple who etch their anxieties and fears into their skin, and they unsettle me. They make me feel so old. I guess I'm angry because I don't like this getting old. The world passing ahead of me until I can't understand it. Home Ec classes replaced with twenty-four-hour cooking shows on a Food Network. Pictures having to go right from the camera to the internet via a cloud.

"I'm going to take some pictures," Tillie says and opens the truck door.

"Okay dear." I open my own door to follow her.

"Let's look around," she calls to the kids in the truck.

I follow the three of them on the path between the line of cars and the steep drop down the hillside to the water. Then a hyper little beagle trailing a leash bolts past with its nose to the dirt. It sprints down into the valley. Several little boys run after it, yelling, "Stop."

Dax bolts after the dog which is surprisingly fast.

"Go help, Randy," Tillie calls to me. I walk down the hill. The beagle is already out of sight and Dax and the kids are about to dip far enough into the shadows there's no sense in me following, but I do anyway. I guess I am no different from any other man my age. In fact, I imagine the lives of men vary only slightly along the same groove—young man, lost man, old man. I hear the dog baying around me and soon lose sight of the trail. I walk along the shore until I find a path back up but that takes a long time and I have to rest along the way.

When I do reach the top Tillie and Nedra sit on the open tailgate. Nedra is crying and Tillie is holding her hand. I can't name what it is, but I know Tillie will want to stay late into the night on the ridge and watch the fires burn. She'll want me to take the long way home, to keep us together as a foursome.

"It's my birthday," she'll say, touching my arm, so I'll slowly drift back into and then through town with the strangers I've gathered who also need safe passage through the drifting smoke and darkest hours.

RECLAMATION

My whole life I've had this feeling at my core that people wouldn't remember me from one meeting to the next and was surprised, even touched, if they did. Looking back, I kept clear of people because of this and spent much of my youth in solitary endeavors. I hunted fossils and Iroquois arrowheads along the shores of Lake Erie, framed my own kites from balsa and tarps, and started my own fish tank to breed tropical lionfish. All this to say, I was a lonely boy. So to have had a friend—any friend, when younger—perhaps bound me to give over part of myself and follow wherever they led.

At the Boys & Girls Club during a pickup basketball game, Horby, who played with anger and grace, was on my team. He was confident in his movements and thus his body, unafraid to play skins, where I hated having to reveal my pudgy belly that would ride me all of my days.

During our game, a kid named Kenneth York called me "a bucket of love butter" and slapped my bare stomach so hard it left a deep purple handprint blooming across my navel. Horby for some reason stood up for me, and in the ensuing scuffle, Kenneth lost a bucket of blood from his chin. Horby got suspended from the club for two months but left with my undying gratitude. From then on, I became his willing lackey, a lieutenant in all his headlong, half-cocked efforts to remold his world to the one he felt he was due.

After leaving the club, we ended up at Horby's. He lived in a small ranch house outside of Dunkirk on the downslope running into Lake Erie, which is sixty foot deep but churns up thirty-foot swells on foul nights. At the high end of the hill, Interstate 90 makes a deep oxbow between Erie, Pennsylvania, and Buffalo, New York. A vineyard surrounded the home. Neat rows of hardy vines clung to the sand-and-gravel soil and grew despite the winds and winters.

He and his older brothers, Ronny and Micha, were being raised by his Uncle Jeremy, who lived on VA disability checks and random fill-in holiday shifts at the Whetstone Knife factory. He sold rocks he painted in different patterns at a monthly farmers market but once in a while sort of lost his mind and tossed those rocks through neighborhood windows until the police came and arrested him. I never had the courage to ask why they lived with their uncle.

Uncle Jeremy barbecued us hamburgers on a rusty grill on my first visit. He opened the screen door and yelled inside, "Boys. Tammy. Dinner."

The two brothers and a woman in a long T-shirt covering her underwear came out to join us. It was almost six at night, but she'd been sleeping. There was a scar on her thigh that looked like fire tongs, and she'd had a hot coal tattooed between the prongs. We all sat around the patio on folding chairs and ate as the sunlight pulled back from the vineyard, which struck me as somehow both wild and tamed. I ate my burger in silence but kept peeking glances at Tammy's tattoo.

We finished eating, and Horby took me to his room and let me in on his scheme to make money selling puppies. I had made some money from my paper route and seeded it to adopt an all-white female boxer he'd seen at the local kennel.

The next time I went to the house, a small white female boxer whimpered in a dog cage. Micha drove up with a second dog, another white boxer. This one a male.

"We'll mate 'em," Horby said.

At first the dogs snarled at each other, but soon, after snipping, the male mounted the female. It was over fast, but they got stuck together and somehow ended up ass to ass with both of them howling, as if one was being birthed from the other.

"Is this part of it?" I asked.

Jeremy ran around the corner after hearing the awful dog noises. "Hose 'em off!" he yelled.

Once the dogs separated, we took the male back to its home. Horby knocked on the door. An older woman answered. He told her he recognized the dog from this house and had found it loose and scared down the road. He petted its head and acted concerned until the lady gave us a reward of twenty dollars each.

"Not bad, right?" He pocketed both the twenties.

When the female boxer never got pregnant, he tried a new tack. He had Jeremy adopt a pregnant dog from the kennel. This dog was a giant Irish Wolfhound mix. Jeremy moved padlocked military lockers around and built a den for it in his garage. Once the pups came, the giant mother sat atop an old army trunk and growled over her pups like a demonic gargoyle and wouldn't let anyone near.

Despite this, he borrowed my lawn mowing money to put an advertisement in the local paper's trade pages: *Irish Wolf Hound*

Puppies for Sale. Full Breed. $350 dollars each.

This brought three interested parties. One paid for the mutt in full, another bargained us down to $200, and the third saw the pups and walked off without another word. $550 was a fortune to us, and though there was now a white boxer, a giant wolfhound, and three of its growing puppies, it felt like a success. Jeremy befriended them all, feeding them and letting them live in his garage when they weren't free-ranging over the neighboring vineyards.

Jeremy had been in the first Gulf War. His hair had inexplicably fallen out while there, and he had had health issues ever since.

"They gassed him," Horby told me.

"Who?"

"Saddam Hussein. Or the US Army tested something on him. No one knows. A bunch of those guys are getting sick."

Over our Christmas break, Tammy called Jeremy from downtown and said a dog stuck on an ice floe had drifted out into the lake. We helped launch Jeremy's small skiff into the lake, where we all headed out past the ice buildup to the rocking open water to the east. My dad, whom I no longer saw, worked as a furniture salesman in a dying department store. The job suited him, his energy levels. No one ever called him to be of help for random calamities.

A dark spot shifted on a breakaway ice floe. The animal's piercing yellow eyes flashed back at our lights. Icicles dripped off its ears, and as we got closer, it started snapping its teeth.

"Not a dog, boys."

The coyote trembled.

Horby made a hand signal to bring the boat alongside the ice. Then he made a peace symbol to the animal as Jeremy eased the throttle and turned the boat. I scooted up next to him, leaving the middle of the skiff empty.

"Now or never," Jeremy said.

The coyote crouched as it took a few steps into the skiff and curled on the deck. Jeremy throttled full-tilt back to shore. Wind worked at the coyote's fur as I imagined the infections that could come from its bite. When we dragged the skiff onto the shore ice, where I half expected the animal to join the vineyard pack, it jumped out and ran away.

In January, Jeremy walked into the local Arby's and flipped out about the lights being on too bright. He made such a scene that the police came, which led to a trip to the VA hospital. He came home with a manila envelope of pictures of an inoperable brain tumor the size of a plum. Soon after, Tammy stopped coming around.

When Lake Erie froze over, we brought skates to the water's edge, walked out past heaved ice shoals, and laced up where the lake became a smooth sheet. With our shoes dangling around our necks by the tied shoelaces, we ventured out into the darkening night. Horby, of course, was faster than I was and skated like he intended to glide all the way past the ship channel to Ontario.

It was exhilarating to be out in the night air with the scratching "Who-it, Who-it" of the blades on ice the only sound beyond my own heartbeat. I expected the ice to be clear, glassine enough to see sixty feet below, but it was windswept and splintered. White cracks branched out in every direction like captured lighting strikes. Sudden heaves of ice walls rose four feet tall, and we slid up to them and dove onto the raised sheet and skated farther into the lake.

Long past when I wanted to turn back, light faded from the sky, and a brilliant cluster of stars spread out overhead. My legs burned, but I shut my eyes and gave myself over to the rhythm of gliding through the dark, which is a sensation I've longed for ever since. We came upon a series of darkened fishing huts closer to shore, so I knew we'd doubled back without my realizing. The sight of the huts filled me with terror. I had no idea where I was out on the lake but blindly followed someone else, like in a way I didn't matter.

Horby went closer to the huts. I took a rest but was overcome by an unease, as if I were being watched. It made me restless and hyperalert to the night, the marbled cracks in the ice, stars filling the sky. Above us, the Milky Way, another heaved-up wall of light. Everything scared me, as if I was about to fall upward into the sky or crash through the ice. Both were equally cold and expansive. I stood there amazed for a long time before the "Who-it, Who-it" of his skating toward me broke my reverie.

"Go. Go." His arms were full of fishing poles and one huge tackle box stolen from the huts.

In the spring, Jeremy started losing weight. Horby biked around town to older people's homes and helped them organize garage sales, where he took the first look through their junk to hunt out the random valuable stuff himself, then placed ads to sell the pilfered items as antiques. This ended up with heaps of useless crap tossed onto an epic bonfire in the vineyard. Truckers passing by on the highway must have slowed as they passed, wondering if it were a home set ablaze, some life altered forever.

In one of the garage sales I helped him set up, I found an old history book all about explorers, starting as far back as there were stories. Troglodytes venturing from caves, Egyptian river merchants,

Phoenicians, Alexander the Great, Hannibal crossing the Alps, Roman legions, the Silk Road, then the Vikings and Genghis Khan. I spent all summer reading that book. I thrilled to the flow of adventures but also to the fact they each had known endings. The lives and events had all been passed down and recorded and could be followed to a conclusion, which, I think now, was what appealed to me more than any adventure.

Everything in my own life was out of my control. I had no sense of how it would end. Reading that book when I was home and going to Horby's to avoid my own home kept me from getting swamped in the wake of my parents' domestic eruption. The endless nights of them weeping behind their bedroom doors, resentful of each other's frailties. I don't know of any betrayals. They were simply mismatched people. At some point, I was not glue enough, which brought such a sense of shame that I folded into myself and lost any outward character or presence. I'd been too frightened by the whole ordeal. If I stayed quiet, out of the way, at least I wouldn't make anything worse.

Horby and I climbed a giant radio tower to get a better look at the great lake fleet far out in the water. Once we got to the top, we spooked a huge group of pigeons nested there, and dozens of them splattered us. I screamed and almost fell.

Looking out from the tower, I thought about how my father had kept a shortwave radio as a boy and listened for voices from different parts of the country. He'd stick pins in the map of where he'd picked up transmissions from, amazed at how far the voices traveled. He gave me a big map like it, and I used it, but to track all the places the characters in the books I read lived or traveled. Sometimes, if I loved a book, I'd wrap a string around the pin and wire it from pin to pin across the map. Perhaps we were both dreaming of larger worlds, but in our own ways. Both of us most likely meek, gentle boys.

I thought of all the radio waves passing over and through us while up in the tower and looked out at the roads other people chose to get out of town. Horby took change out of his pocket and looked down.

"Heads or tails."

The coin flipped outward, flashing and disappearing over and over until we could not track it below.

"Two out of three." He flipped another.

"Three out of five."

I could not see any of them land.

"Jeremy told us he won't live out the year," Horby said and kept flipping coins out into the air.

Jeremy became too thin. Ronny got kicked out of high school for selling pot and took a job working as a roofer in Salamanca, near the Indian reservation. Micha was a senior in high school for the second time. Horby, who must have internalized the weight of debt, was becoming an entrepreneur, certain that no matter the quantity or scale of his failures, he would finally succeed.

He went back to the newspaper and paid for ads selling things he did not own: remote-control cars, fishing poles, and frog-growing kits, listing a PO box he rented to receive payments that never came. No matter. He still advertised tires, car parts, and sling shots.

He kept himself busy scheming, I think, because the speed at which Jeremy began spiraling down was too much for him. After an incident late in spring, Jeremy went from the police station again to the hospital and was put in intensive care. He pulled through after a week, then came home gaunt but focused.

"We need a plan," he kept saying. "A plan."

In my mind, I was the fourth brother. Privy to everything.

"I can't go into care, or you'll go into care." Jeremy pointed at Horby. "You'll go into a system. Your brothers will be too young to take you in court, so we'll not let it happen. Need a plan."

He paced around the room; it came off as an odd waddle. I kept taking in the sway of his shadow. "And the VA checks. We'll need those to keep coming after." He looked at me. "Maybe time you head home, pal," he said, which hurt as much as my parents telling me they were getting divorced all over again.

"Sure, sure." I tried to hide the sting of not belonging and just barely made it outside before crying. The dogs ran through the vines howling on the hillside.

All summer, Jeremy quit shaving and his beard grew into a scraggly graying mess. He grew skinny, moved slower, but kept busy in the garage, which we were no longer allowed into. He came out covered with dirt carrying shovels and pickaxes and drank huge swallows of water from the green garden hose before rinsing off his dirt-caked arms.

"What's he doing?" I asked but never got an answer.

Before the grape harvest, I biked down the hill to Horby's house, seeking sanctuary from my family, my solitude.

"Now's not a good time," Ronny said.

Submitting to him right away, I turned to leave, but Horby walked out.

"Can he stay?"

Micha followed him out and nodded. "Come on. You can help."

I followed them into the house. We went to Jeremy's room. The lights were on. Jeremy was laid out on his bed in his military uniform. Not moving. Some primordial chill rose from my chest.

"This morning," Horby said.

I took a step back but bumped into Micha, who put a hand on my shoulder. "You'll help. You won't tell anyone. Ever."

I nodded without daring to look at any of them. Jeremy was clean-shaven, and his hair had been combed.

It got dark. We lifted the sheet Jeremy was on off the bed and laid it on a rug. The older brothers wrapped him in the rug, and we brought the rug to the garage. The four of us his pallbearers. Inside the garage, a deep, meticulous grave was dug from the dirt floor. We laid the rug down next to the hole.

"Jeremy dug it. He made it longer and deeper than needed," Micha told me.

"He said he wanted room to move around down there," Ronny said.

Micha and Ronny walked out of the garage.

The brothers came back with baskets of grapes picked from the hillside. The white boxer and one of the Irish wolfhounds followed and sniffed at the doorway.

We lowered Jeremy in, then each dropped bunches of grapes into the grave, shoveled the heaping pile of sand, gravel, and loam over him. Once the rest of the dirt had been swept away and there was no sign of Jeremy's final resting place, we all went outside, where we sat for hours until the sun began to rise over the lake.

What did I know then of sacrifice? Of military honors Jeremy would have had. Of a lonely, self-dug grave and dying in secret to keep a nephew in the home he knew. To keep money coming to those boys for a few more years, enough to get them clear into legal adulthood. What did I know of washing, shaving, and dressing a dead man?

I went home bound by a secret hiding on that hillside. I was exhausted and went to sleep most of the day, unnoticed by my mother, who was at work, then came home exhausted from working.

Not long after this, Horby stopped calling me to come over to his house or to help him with some new money-making idea.

"Can we do something after school?" I asked him in the hallway one day.

"No," he said and walked away.

I didn't know what to do with myself because of this, but by some grace soon became intoxicated by the powdered sugar of first love, a curly-haired girl who once took a gulp of ice water, held it in her mouth, and kissed my bare shoulder. The sensation possessed me, and I found it easy to turn toward a new source of attention, one offering light and love.

After high school, I moved to Buffalo for a community college associate's degree, then earned a scholarship to the University of Buffalo. I stopped going home and did not see Horby for many years, though I heard about him.

From what I pieced together over the next decades, he built docks along Chautauqua Lake and Lake Erie. For a while, his brothers worked with him. They started hiring guys from the reservation who worked like mad, and together they put other shoreline contracting companies out of business.

There was an incident. A competitor showed up to a dock site and started causing trouble, degrading the Salamanca crew until Horby pulled a military-grade machine gun out of his truck, one that had most likely come from Jeremy's old locker, and shot up the competitor's truck. The judge who oversaw the case had a half-finished dock on his lakefront home, which Horby would not complete until the case was thrown out.

When that dock company was built and began dredging sand from out in the lake and pumping it ashore to make private beaches, it made enough money to run itself. He left Ronny in charge of it, and went on to start a home construction business. He made a fortune throwing up suburban developments and ran that with Micah. When I do think of him, I always wonder if he ever looked back at himself with a rush of shame, the way the smallest slights endlessly eddy in my own imagination.

I became a history teacher at a high school outside DC which offers a middle-class existence I am happy to have. Like the book I'd found on explorers all those years ago, I found comfort in the truths people have gone out to find but, more importantly, brought back to help make sense of the world. In a way, that sense of history, of looking back, has sustained me. But it has also kept me from looking at the life unfolding around me in the way it deserved.

"You're empty. You don't engage," my wife said during an argument when she was tired of me. "You hide in your books. It's like you're not a full person."

The words hurt her to say, but I felt the intensity of their truth. The weight of that truth scared me with its potential to lead us into a dim, miserable room, arguing ourselves out, the way my parents did. The fight led me to promises of taking more agency in my day-to-day life, and in our marriage. Though this meant I needed to look backward for what I had lost, or forward when I became uncertain in my own feelings.

Soon after my wife and I fought, there was talk that my father needed to be checked on, to see if it was time for him to go into assisted living. I used it as an excuse to fly back to Buffalo, then rented a car, and drove toward the gray towns of my youth. Olean, Jamestown, and Dunkirk. The rustic, rusty beauty of those strange places and the lake, lurking in the dark along I-90, was so familiar.

First came a hard talk with my father about his future and mine. Where the pins in the map would lead us. Then I drove to see my mother and asked her how she had come to terms with her grief. I never knew to ask until then. I reported all these talks back to my wife at night, and it felt like a confession, some part of myself I'd sealed away out of shame, or fidelity to everyone I'd ever loved.

The next morning, I drove past a billboard for Whetstone Knives. A giant gleaming blade fell toward a glossy walnut cutting board, but from a distance the blade looked to be cutting the field behind it in half. To me the image felt an apt metaphor for my trip, cleaving history and hope into two factions. Yet the place still felt so deep with chaos, confusion, and confluence. I drove on to Uncle Jeremy's house. From the high turnoff of the highway, the dry husks of last summer's crop shriveled on the rows of posts and wires. The rows now ran right over where the house had been. Beyond the vineyard, the lake was starting that ancient cooling process that would soon freeze it over. I took pictures of the field and the shore to show my wife. I'd tell her about my time as a beachcombing isolate, and then about Horby, which was why I'd really come back.

Horby's construction office was a brick building with a dozen construction vans parked along the side. Inside was a waiting room with a receptionist.

"Tell him an old friend is here to visit," I told the receptionist and gave my name.

An enormous geode crystal filled the front of his office. As I waited, unsure if he'd come meet me, I imagined crawling into the crystal and tilting it onto my back like a shell. Who would have unearthed such a stone, the little pin-hammer strike of discovery? The awe that must have come when they found it. Or, in this case, it could have been scavenged from an estate sale and polished for effect.

I didn't know what kind of man he'd become, but I guessed the foundation of his character was settling during our time together. There were things I wanted to tell him. I'd come to talk about history, connections, mythmaking, and one rugged place the passage of time had allowed us both to climb out of.

"I'm afraid he's not available," the receptionist told me after several minutes of giving yes or no answers on her phone.

"Okay. I can wait all day."

"I'm afraid he's not available today."

Several workers came in carrying clipboards and lunch boxes.

My own sensibility nudged me to tell Horby that I had become a bank of old memories. Horby, who at least on this day would not let the memory of his life and its collection of human struggles slow him down.

"Please tell him I came to talk about when we were younger. How I have nothing but good memories."

I left the building, walked around the side, and saw a haggard version of a face I once knew. Micha lumbered toward me with work boots, jeans, a white button-down shirt, and navy blazer. He was holding a mug of coffee. His hair was wet and combed, but his eyes looked red and hungover. He was looking at me, trying to place me, and the moment he did, he stopped walking and stared.

"Hello," I said.

He nodded.

"I was back visiting my family. Thought I'd say hello to your brother."

"Did you catch him?"

"No."

"What did you need to talk about?"

"I looked down on your old home. It's all vineyard now."

"Yeah. I know. Our crew did that."

"Well. It's a beautiful spot."

"It is," Micha said, apprehensive about my presence.

"I wanted to tell your brother I thought your uncle Jeremy was sublimely generous. I think it may have been the best attribute of anyone I've ever come across."

"I'll tell him,"

Micah walked into the building. I sat in the rental car across the street telling my wife on the phone that I hadn't seen him. Then Micha and Horby exited the back of the building and got into a van. Horby's hair was still towhead white, cut short, and slicked back. He was thicker around the chest, but his face was still sharp, forever recognizable. Their van pulled out, and before Micha shifted forward, I locked eyes with Horby who was in the passenger seat. He nodded. I gave him a small, short wave, then switched to a peace sign.

As they turned and drove away, I was pulled back to the memory of Horby out skating on the ice as it grew dark and then became night with the launching of a star-ridden sky as clear as any I'd ever seen. I felt that intimacy of being humbled by something greater than me that I did not yet know I was starved for. Though as Horby skated toward the battened-down fishing huts and began to cut along their base where he could slide inside to root around for valuables, I realized it was the magnitude of the lake and sky that offered me comfort. That strangeness of being on the ice at night, an explorer, uncertain if I'd be forever faceless beneath the sprawl of stars and time or eventually make it back with a story to tell.

Acknowledgments

Waiting For The Coywolf, *The Sun*

Sugar And Priscilla, *Yemasee*

Levi's Recession, *Glimmer Train And New Stories From The Midwest*

How We Disappear, *War, Literature, And The Arts*

The Names Of Wind, *Zone 3*

The Brooks Range, Printer's Row, *The Chicago Tribune*

Unbend The River, *Sundial Magazine*

Red. Off. Red. Off. *Secondhand Stories Podcast*

Reclamation, *The Missouri Review*

© Megan Bearder

DEVIN MURPHY is a national bestselling author of the novels *The Boat Runner* and *Tiny Americans*, published by Harper Perennial. These books have been selected as Barnes & Noble Discover New Writers, Illinois Reads, and book of the year by the Chicago Writer's Association, and Society of Midland Authors. His recent work appears in *The Chicago Tribune*, *The Missouri Review*, *The Sun*, and *Outside Magazine* as well as many others. He holds a BA and MA from St. Bonaventure University, an MFA from Colorado State University, a PhD from the University of Nebraska-Lincoln, is a Professor of Creative Writing at Bradley University, and lives in Chicago with his wife and their three kids.